Interstice Undone

An Epic Crossover

J.J. Johnson
Jason C. Joyner
Steve Rzasa

Essential Reading

J.J. Johnson (Iggy & Oz)

Iggy and Oz: The Plastic Dinos of Doom
Iggy and Oz: The Soda Pop Wars
Iggy and Oz: The Living Snot
Iggy and Oz: The Great Ice Cream Truck Heist

https://jjjohnsonwrites.com/

Jason C. Joyner (The Anointed)

Launch
Fractures
Anointed

https://www.jasoncjoyner.com/

Steve Rzasa (Mercury Hale)

Mercury on Guard
Mercury for Hire
Mercury at Risk
Mercury is Hot
Mercury out Cold
Mercury off Course
Mercury with Style

https://steverzasa.com/

This is where the fun begins...

It was June of 2020.

The world was in the midst of a pandemic that up-ended everybody's lives. My writing buddy Jason Joyner and I had been commiserating via Facebook Messenger about various and sundry things. Next thing I know, he messaged, "I just had inspiration on how to start an Anointed/Mercury crossover."

Me: "Ooh watcha got?"

Jason: "Just Harry picking up something weird in the interdimensional space that he ports within."

Me: "Sounds cool!" (*Note: This is my default response to cool ideas.)

Jason: "What kind of trouble could they all get into?"

Me: "Hmm. Maybe Harry could see an astral fiend, convince others to go after a monster? Wind up in San Camillo? Or Mercury follows a fiend to them?"

And on the discussion went. The plot didn't end up quite like that but it was enough of a seed to plant that, for two years, it germinated in both of our minds. Meanwhile I had started writing a massive military sci-fi series with Daniel Gibbs and by the time I finished penning the last book, I was switching back over to my Interstice universe writings—which meant I was daydreaming about Mercury Hale. I must have had a flash of inspiration or a brain fart, because I messaged him, "I was just realizing… Your Anointed series was in San Francisco, right? Mercury's chasing monsters up in a fictional part of Northern California. I'm dyyyying for us (and JJ) to cross over our characters, even if it's a fan project that never sees the light of day publication wise!"

I kept remembering Jason's original idea, and by then J.J.'s Iggy and Oz had already established themselves in the same story world as Mercury.

That got Jason's brain churning, and a couple of weeks later he wrote me back, "I may have started writing a scene with my characters at a ren faire until Harry ports them through a weird cloud? or something and they do their first interdimensional travel …"

Me: "Yessss love it!"

Jason soon formed another chat called "Epic Crossover!" and we began planning in earnest, once we dragged J.J. in. He was totally on board but he did have to run copyright questions past Iggy, who, let's face it, hadn't made it out of middle school yet. The next year and a half were a blur of us writing while our lives continued onward, including two Realm Makers' writing conferences (IYKYK).

In spite of the challenges, all of a sudden it was the end

of October 2023, and we had done what we didn't know was possible—turn a crazy idea of merging three sets of heroes from three different series intended for children, teens, and adults into a cohesive (mostly) and highly entertaining (for sure!) novella.

We hope you enjoy it.

-   Steve Rzasa, Spring 2024

Chapter One

Demarcus Bartlett

Demarcus raised his staff in defense, barely able to parry the blow from another weapon. *If only I could use my super speed.* He spun back, his leather boots slipping on the worn-down grass. His opponent unleashed another vicious swing, taking Demarcus in the midsection.

A kill shot, if the weapon hadn't been a well-rendered foam replica.

Still, the strike forced the air from his lungs. He stood, holding his belly as his adversary raised a costume face plate and beamed at him.

"Good attempt, worthy foe. You will have to train harder to fight Sir Quinlan of the Shire," the man said, offering his hand to shake.

Demarcus smiled back, imagining the way he could destroy this guy if he could let his true ability show. "You too, man. I've got some practice to keep up."

He offered his foam staff to the next person in line while he scanned the crowd for his friends. Coming to the renaissance fair was Sarah Jane's idea. Since she was usually the quiet one who went along with the others' suggestions, they all agreed to join fully in the fun. But wearing a tunic, breeches, and boots rented from the costume shop felt a bit off to him. Where were his regal West African Manding robes instead?

Wandering through the colorful crowd, he walked past stands of merchants hawking different wares. The scent of candles mixed with leather as cheery folk traded for jewelry and weapons with their phone pay apps. Demarcus chuckled at the irony.

His nose led him to the delicious odors of roasting beef and the food vendors. Not surprisingly, he found Harry gnawing on a leg of turkey. It probably didn't taste as good with all the fake beard fibers caught in his mouth.

"Pleth. How do guys eat with a beard?" Harry said through a bite. His wizard robe looked sick, but his red hair clashed with the white beard, which was now stained with drippings.

"You know you could pull the beard down for meals? You don't have to be authentic the whole time."

Harry put a hand to his chest in outrage. "Forsooth! What wickedness you speak."

"Sorry bro, but you're not a Potter or any other kind of

wizard," Demarcus replied with a raised eyebrow.

Now a grin broke out. "I do have a pretty cool trick."

Demarcus sighed. "Yeah, so do I, but we're here for down time. No powers today . . . unless we can't find the girls. Have you seen them?"

Before an answer came, a rubber dagger poked into Demarcus's back. He yelped and twisted around, almost using his speed. Sarah Jane stood with the widest smile on her face. "You couldn't find us, but we found you."

Demarcus wondered why she had dressed like a thief. Her black hood hid reddish-blonde hair, while a fake leather tunic and leggings finished the look. Guess she was good at sneaking. He didn't even see her coming.

A blonde beauty in a peasant dress strode over, laughing. Demarcus would always have stomach flips when hearing Lily's voice. His girlfriend kept pointing at him, barely holding it together.

"She got you so good!" she finally said when the laughs died down. "You jumped so high."

His cheeks warmed with the teasing and her drawing close. He cleared his throat. "Why did you dress as a thief? It seems out of character for you."

Sarah Jane did a little curtsy. "That's the point. I can role play something else at things like the ren faire. Everyone expects a shy SJ. Well, here I get to express myself in a way I don't feel comfortable doing otherwise."

Demarcus noticed Harry's googly eyes locked onto his crush. It worked well for the Anointed that both sets of guys and girls were couples—but would it cause problems if either of them broke up? They all wanted to honor God with their divine gifts and in their relationships.

The sounds of Irish flutes and mandolins floated through the air as their group passed an arch of flowers where a jester was entertaining kids. If they wanted to see the jousting competition, they'd need to find spots soon. The reputation for this show was widespread around the Bay Area.

He tried to catch Lily's hand, but she pulled her phone out of her belt where she had it tucked. Shoot—he had to be quicker next time. She read a text message and glanced at him.

"Kashvi's back in San Jose with her family. She's planning on meeting up with us next weekend. But she said a weird fog is rolling in. It wouldn't respond to her water bending," Lily frowned.

Their former adversary turned friend was ready to start training with their group. If she said something was fishy with anything involving water, they'd best pay attention. In fact, he noticed the air turning hazy around the faire too. San Francisco got fog routinely, but this far south they didn't see it as often.

The air closed in around them, making Demarcus's

hair on the back of his neck stand. The others reacted as well. Even Harry stopped nibbling his turkey leg to look around.

Sarah Jane crouched a little, becoming more like a thief with the motion. "Does anyone else think something is going on?" Her eyes widened.

The fog thickened enough that they had to stop, not able to see where they were going. Lily tried a quick flash of her light, but it just reflected off the mist. Demarcus thought of their battle with the Hoshek, where the evil spirit had been vanquished at a high cost. Could something similar be happening?

"Anyone think we should get our gear and investigate?" Demarcus whispered. They all voiced their assent. "Okay then. The faire will have to wait. Harry, can you take us to the room?" They had a special room at their church where they kept their gear and supersuits.

Harry nodded and offered a greasy hand to Sarah Jane. She stuck her tongue out in disgust but knew he would hold on to the turkey as long as possible. Lily took her hand then locked fingers with Demarcus. Now Harry could port them quietly away, and they'd see if anything weird was going on.

The air warped around them—and then the world turned inside out.

Normally it was a blip. One moment they would be in

the park, and the next they'd pop up in the youth room. When Harry first ported someone, they usually got sick to their stomach.

This time Demarcus's body stretched and swirled like he was circling down a drain. Lily's scream both filled his ears and sounded like it echoed from far away. Their hands stayed locked together as they tumbled, spun, and careened through a strange space with neon lights and weird shapes until Demarcus blacked out.

Lying on cool grass, Demarcus first noticed screams of people nearby. Was something happening at the ren faire? He tried to straighten out, but his body felt like he'd done CrossFit for eight hours. Groaning, he noticed the smell of something familiar.

Pepperoni pizza?

A face appeared, blurry to Demarcus's spinning eyes. A man's voice said, "You okay?"

He held a living lightning bolt in his hand.

Chapter Two

Mercury Hale

Okay, look. I might have been rude with the kids but in my defense, I wasn't in the best mood.

I'd been carrying pizza back from Carlito's II when the playground equipment tried to strangle me.

The city of San Camillo was never gonna finish Century Park, pandemic-related construction delay or not, but that didn't stop the center of my fast-food universe from opening a satellite takeout joint in the same neighborhood north of its home location. I swore the pepperoni pizza there was even better than the original's, but I'd never tell Carlito.

Just because I cut through the broken chain-link fence meant to keep out trespassers didn't mean I deserved to get mauled by a jungle gym.

No joke, the skeletal dome of yellow and red tubes came unzipped. It lashed out with a rubberized grip meant to make it easier for seven-year-olds to climb. Turned out that same grip also made it easier to throttle me.

I acted on reflex: dropped the pizza box, pulled the pulsar stave from under my shirt, willed it to life so it sizzled like the summer sun, and sliced through the offending appendage.

I pulled the rest free from my neck. "So much for Vacation: Take Two," I muttered.

The gym re-formed into a gnarled, twisted mass of rubber-coated metal. It groaned and squealed like someone—three guesses who—had tried to make an astral fiend out of it. I wondered if the Whisperer had gotten bored of his usual reach-across-the-Interstice-and-try-to-kill-me attacks. Definitely weird. Weirdest thing I'd ever seen? Not even close.

Of course, the fog oozing up out of the stacked sod was weirder. San Camillo gets fog, sure, even in the summer, but not like that—not as fast or localized. I mean, it refused to spread beyond the chain link fence.

Then the lightning started. Purple lightning.

That did it. I slapped my earbud, way too hard. My earlobe stung, but Aerosmith cut out and my direct secure line to Procyon Foundation's secret Tracking office rang.

"Mercury! Oh, hi. How's your vacation going? I wasn't going to bother you but I sent out Drone Four to check out some really fascinating readings coming out of Century

Park that started out tachyonic but if they—"

"Hey, Liz," I cut in. "I'm there and I've got a monster jungle gym on the attack and an entire pepperoni pizza pie on the ground, so A., I know, and B., we've got to contain this."

"You are? You do?" Liz Stojan sounded concerned but not startled. Like I said, not the weirdest thing. "I'm re-tasking our response team."

She'd better do it soon. The park was socked in so badly I couldn't see the buildings around the block but could hear the monster shriek—and people scream. If that thing could feed off their energy like a real astral fiend . . .

Two more modified monkey bars shot out of the mist. I ducked one, spun aside, and severed the other. The stave flashed like a lighthouse beacon, spraying gold and white sparks where it cut the metal. "Liz!"

"Oh! Okay. Um . . ." She sounded like she was chewing her lip. "Our team is on the way. There's no rip nearby, at least, nothing that matches what we're used to seeing, but I am registering a dimensional flux similar to what we saw at Echelon Plaza last month, or even earlier than that, when the astral fiend merged with the arachnafury from the other dimension."

I frowned. The astral fury? The giant fireball-spider? It had mutated out of a rift that opened between here and the fantasy land—

A body slammed into me. Make that four bodies, one after each other. I hit a stack of sod.

Something cardboard and greasy broke the rest of my fall. Yeah, I'd sat on my pizza.

I sighed. The heavenly aroma of marinara, mozzarella, and pepperoni filled the air. The gym-beast groaned with metallic dismay.

"Tell me about it," I said.

"Um, Mercury? The best I can guess is we're seeing multiple dimensional intersections at once. Cyril can't give me how many or which ones because the analysis is sending him into a loop." Liz sounded pissed, as she was prone to sound when anything injured her favorite supercomputer.

At least she hadn't sat in her lunch. Did she have any idea how much a pizza pie cost these days?

The monster churned the earth, and even though people were still yelling, the fog had flattened out enough I could tell none were visible nearby. Cool. Nobody dead and no clear witnesses. Yet.

I glanced back to see what boneheads had run into me and found more medieval heroes.

I say "more" because a few years ago I'd had a visit from an ice sorcerer named Bowen and his katana-wielding, smart-mouth sidekick Niall. They'd come from the same fantasy dimension as the giant flaming spider, a place where magic and myth were the norm. Great warriors. Terrible dressers.

These teenagers wore the same kinds of clothing.

I leaned over and offered a hand to a black kid. "You okay?"

"I'm—huh?" He ran a hand through his dreads. "What happened to us? Harry?"

A thin redheaded boy sat up. He spat grass from his mouth. "I don't know, but this isn't the room. I thought I smelled the ocean—"

"Yeah, we're outside." I scowled. "Do they not have that back home?"

The redhead's eyes widened. "You've . . . That's a weapon?"

Oh, right. The stave. Yeah, I still held it, and yeah, at its full power, it looked like living lightning instead of a brass and silver cylinder.

The black kid was up in a flash—like *the* Flash. I mean, one second, he was flat on his back. The next, he was braced in front of his pal, arms spread, his expression one of defiance, but he didn't look the least bit afraid. A blast of wind hit me a second later. "Back off, man."

I held out both hands in a friendly gesture. "Hang on. I'm guessing your buddy isn't a werefox, then, is he?"

Blinding light bathed the entire scene.

"Lily, look out! That guy might be working with the *Ar-*

chai!"

"I've never seen one with a staff like that, Demarcus." That came from a blonde girl—at least, I think she was blonde. The light blobs I couldn't blink away made identifying anyone difficult.

The gym-beast picked then to hook my leg with a metal loop. I slammed face-first into the grass. The beast pulled me into the mist, my fingers dragging ruts in the dirt like I was the next victim in a Sam Raimi horror flick. Must have looked terrifying because Lily screamed.

I couldn't blame her. The monster held me upside down. I twisted so I could face it. Whatever forces from the Interstice that had brought the gym-beast to life had a flair for the dramatic. They'd formed a swirling black void speckled with diamond stars and purple lightning in the middle of the tangled metal and plastic mass. The creature howled at me. Sounded like a strident foghorn with metal scraping at the edges.

The pulsar stave lay ten feet away. Because of course it did.

Joke was on the monster. I had a reservoir of the same extradimensional energies the stave channeled pooled in my prosthetic leg. It blazed gold. "Hands off, ugly." I swung upward with a kick that dislodged its grip.

More twisted metal, stripped of its plastic, shot toward my face. I dropped, feeling like everything was in slow-motion, which let me focus on not just on the monster but on who the heck the kids were.

The monster's remaining arms jabbed down at a girl with auburn hair. Harry the redhead cried out, "Sarah Jane!"

Lily held out her hands like she was gonna singlehandedly end the attack.

Demarcus ran for me. And I mean, ran. Normal speed. Which was weird because he wasn't slowed down by everyone else. Instead, he sprinted faster than I'd ever managed even when amped up with the stave's power.

He caught me and we turned into a heap of four arms and four legs.

"Move it, kid!" I reached for the stave but came up short by inches. The monster's arm whisked through the air dead overhead.

The stave flashed inches past my ear and lopped off a four-foot chunk of mutated monkey bar that sizzled where the stave's energies turned the metal molten.

The monster screamed. Demarcus stared at my weapon in his hand. I stared at Demarcus, who shouldn't be able to use the stave, and the stave that was supposed to be an inert brass and silver rod.

I yanked it from his hand and pointed at his face. "Stay put. First I kill that thing, then we talk."

When the irate monster snagged me again, I let it take

me. It was a lot clingier than an astral fiend, but as a bonus, it didn't drain me. Didn't feel the slightest bit cold.

It just dragged me toward a gaping mouth-slash-portal ringed with jagged metal.

I willed every ounce of the state's power to life and drained the last of my reservoir. "Hope you're hungry," I growled.

I broke the stave into its two halves and lunged for the center. The stars and lightning battered my senses.

But everything blew up in a blast of icy air when I struck its maw just inside the boundaries.

I wound up on my backside, one last time. Bruises? Check. Damp.

The kids crowded around me. I gazed up at them.

"Mercury!" Liz's cry made me jump. "I saw the footage from Drone Four! Who are they?"

I shook my head. "No clue, but you'd better clear your schedule. I'm bringing them home."

"We're not going anywhere with you until you tell us what just happened." Demarcus held Lily's hand. No mistake. He was in charge.

Sirens wailed from the park's surrounding streets. The mist was breaking up. I jerked my thumb. "You want to stay and play twenty questions with San Camillo's finest? Be my guest. But if you want answers, like I do, we're taking a road trip. Anything else?"

They looked at each other as if they were having a silent conference. Harry raised his hand. "Where's San Camillo?"

Chapter Three

Mercury Hale

Garvey drove me and our fun new foursome back to Procyon Foundation's headquarters. I couldn't figure out how the guy dodged traffic as well as he did. What, had Liz rigged the gray SUVs to phase through solid objects?

Nah, probably not. But I'd seen weird enough things in five-ish years of this crazy work that it wouldn't have surprised me if she had.

More likely she was just hacking the traffic lights from here to Bay Avenue. Worked for me. We made it to San Camillo Bay's scenic shoreline in record time.

Garvey navigated past the cinderblock security post. "Ms. Lark says we're supposed to park around the back. There's a lot of prying eyes—her words."

I craned my neck. No joke. I counted forty people lining the foundation's black metal fence line. Half of them held placards that bore varied slogans. Those messages were pretty similar: "Tell us the truth!"

"What truth do they want to know about?" Lily had her nose almost pressed to the glass.

"Procyon Foundation does a lot of good work in the community," I said. "Public housing. Health clinics. Small business grants. But that's not what our core mission is."

"Core mission?" Garvey snorted.

"What?"

"You sound like Ms. Lark, sir."

I chuckled. "Yeah, well, try being married to her, and see if you could resist the jargon rubbing off on you."

"Not me, sir. Got my own wife to keep me in line."

"So, you're hiding things." Demarcus didn't sound impressed. Maybe he was just as worried as I was about how the kid could use the top-secret weapon I owned.

"Look, kid. We have to." The SUV pulled around the backside of the three towers. Our reflection rippled across the glass running up the sides of the seven-story buildings. "How well do you think most people are gonna handle finding out that there's worse monsters than what you saw in the park lurking around between dimensions, ready to kill them in their sleep? They have a hard enough time wrapping their brains around the everyday stuff."

"He's got a point." The redheaded boy, Harry, looked thoughtful as we exited the SUVs and Garvey escorted us to a back door. A couple of Procyon security guys, both built like slightly smaller versions of the mountain Garvey was, and just as shaved bald, waited inside. "Wouldn't most people go crazy if they really believed a bunch of teenagers had superpowers?"

"That's probably why John doesn't have us advertise them," Sarah Jane said. "But I don't understand—what is this place?"

I grinned at her. Okay, so maybe I was ready to brag. "This is our Batcave. Our Fortress of Solitude."

Harry and Demarcus shared a grin. "Cool," Harry cheered while the two girls rolled their eyes in response. Okay, not all of them are comic book fans.

I led the kids up to the seventh floor of Tower Three, where we hid Tracking, Forecasting, and the Manager's office in three pie-slices of square footage. Tracking was the brains of the operations. There wasn't much light inside, but the dozens of display screens glowed enough to make up for it. We had six people set up at desks that made Star Trek consoles look old-fashioned.

Even Demarcus got wide-eyed and silent when he saw the gigantic map of San Camillo on the center monitor.

"Hey! Are they them? I mean, are these the new travelers?" Elizabeth Stojan pushed out of a rolling chair. Spiky pink hair glowed like it had its own implanted LEDs. She'd put on Converse high tops that were the same shade. Her chair crashed into the desk's edge and she jumped like it was a gunshot. "Oh! Hi guys."

"This is Liz. Liz, these are . . ." I frowned. "You guys said you had a code name, right?"

"The Anointed." Lily struck a tone that made it seem like I was the student and she was the teacher. Okay, then.

"This is great! Really great. I couldn't believe it when Mercury said we have travelers from outside our dimension again, which is funny because as often as it happens you'd think I'd be ready for it and honestly, I have an entire file stored in . . ."

"Liz." I could feel a headache coming on. Don't get me wrong. Liz was fantastic at everything she kept track of in her real brain and the artificial one housed in Cyril the supercomputer, but when she got going she could *get going* and you'd better deploy a verbal spike mat to make her slow down. "Two things: What was the deal with that astral fiend-slash-playground monster, and why did these kids show up at the rip in the same moment?"

"Good questions." Liz wrinkled her nose. "Um, I can help you with one of them. So, the rip was pretty standard. Check out the tachyon spike—it's like we've seen before but with a variation in the particle yield that we haven't."

"Okay." I scratched the back of my head. The readouts on her flat screen desk—that also acted like a giant tablet, which was very cool—were full of so many spiky charts that I thought I was watching the stock market. Except more consistent.

"Here?" Liz tapped the screen. She watched for my reaction, eyebrows raised. I think I was supposed to be impressed. "And this?"

I shrugged.

Liz sighed. "Boys and girls," she said to the boys and girls, "if you sign up to work with an organization that secretly handles monsters from other dimensions, maybe crack a book or two on particle physics and theoretical quantum mechanics so the nerds don't have to keep explaining stuff to you."

The teens exchanged worried looks, like they weren't sure which grownup was the authority in the room. I leaned over Liz's tablet. "So, where did they come from?"

"We told you, man." Demarcus sounded as frustrated as I was starting to feel. Which was a lot. "The Bay Area. You know, San Francisco."

"Yeah, but not *this* San Francisco." I tapped one of Liz's techs on the shoulder. The guy grunted. "Bring up the biggest cities in the country on the map."

"Please."

I glanced at him. "Um, please."

He nodded and made a few clicks with his mouse.

White dots appeared across the USA. I pointed. "See anything odd? I mean, besides the fact that none of you have heard of San Camillo."

Sarah Jane was the first to the front. "Um, I count about five cities that don't exist."

"I don't think there is such a thing as Drake City." Lily made a face at the map. "There's nothing that big so close to Boston, is there?"

"Yep, see?" I smiled at Liz. "Another dimension."

Liz rolled her eyes. "We already knew that, Mercury. We'll have Doc Arne run some tests on them—I mean, if they're okay with it."

"Tests using . . . blood?" Harry—who was wearing a fake beard, I realized—gulped.

"Definitely!" Liz said.

The kid looked way too pale. "Easy there, Miss Mad Scientist. Maybe we'd better start with Narang and the scanner," I said to Liz.

"Oh, we already scanned them when you came in." Liz pointed at a silver bar with a black window in it mounted above the doors to Tracking. "I installed it last week."

"Last *week*? And you didn't tell me?"

"Garvey and Anthony said it would be a good way to watch for outside threats." Liz grinned. "And it doesn't stick out. We got a lot of good scans on you. But anyway, these four are kind of a problem."

"Thanks a lot," Demarcus said.

"Easy, guys." I held up my hands. "Small words for me, Liz."

She pointed at Demarcus. "He used the pulsar stave—but that's not possible. He doesn't show any signs of tachyonic interaction like you or Gemini or Airfoil do. I mean, we have to do a full genetic scan, but I doubt he or the others carry the genetic signature needed to make it work."

"What?" It was my turn to give the kids a weird look. They were staying pretty quiet, which was good, considering they'd been flung out of their dimension into ours, and were probably still minors. I didn't even want to think about getting parental consent for complex particle scans. "How's that even work?"

Lily chewed her lip. She made eye contact with the rest of the gang. "Maybe we should tell him."

Demarcus seemed to mull it over. "Guys?"

"We're probably going to need their help to get home." Harry's cheeks reddened. "I've tried a couple of times to teleport since we got to this city and . . . I don't know why it's not working right. I tried to port us home but it's like I bounced off of something."

"They seem to know a lot more than we do about this stuff, Demarcus." Sarah Jane waved at the inner workings of Tracking.

"Okay." Demarcus looked at me. "The easiest way I can explain it is that our powers come from God."

Oh. I glanced at Liz.

"Don't look at me." Liz rubbed at the bridge of her

nose. "This sounds like a question for Lieutenant Ramos."

Chapter Four

Demarcus Bartlett

Demarcus kept glancing around the room, trying to pay attention to the science gal Liz and the big mouth Mercury while they talked about some Lieutenant Ramos. The setup was definitely impressive. Ratchet, the Anointed's own science advisor, would be going nuts right then if he could check out their gear. Procyon seemed to be a legit group, but he couldn't help having a bad feeling about this.

How were he and his friends going to get home, if they truly were in . . . another dimension?

Normally he'd be geeking out about this, but he did promise Mr. Beausoleil he'd have Lily home by 11 P.M. Would interdimensional travel be an acceptable excuse for being late?

Mercury snapped his fingers. "Hey guys, are you following? What do you mean, 'from God'?"

The sound shook Demarcus back to focusing. "The four

of us last year developed these special gifts. We met at Launch, an influencer conference hosted by Simon Mazor. That's where we learned from our mentor that there was a prophecy about people being given abilities to fight a growing evil. So . . . God gave us these gifts."

Mercury blinked, looked at the Procyon crew, then threw up his hands. "Yeah, I got nothing. It is a Ramos thing."

They kept mentioning him. Lily piped up. "What's with Lieutenant Ramos?"

"He's our liaison with the San Camillo Police Department's task force—with a really long acronym I can never keep straight. They work with us on the weird things."

"Sounds like there's more than a couple of weird things going on in your city. I mean, you were battling living playground equipment with your light stick."

He thought Mercury was going to pop a vessel. "Light stick? The pulsar stave is a weapon from my home dimension."

Harry raised his hand. "Is it like a Force user and a lightsaber? Maybe I should try it."

The way Lily and Sarah Jane reacted, Demarcus knew that was a no-go. "Dude, Han used a saber on Hoth. And no, I don't think you should just try it. That thing is wicked intense." He turned towards Liz. "If it helps to understand what's going on, I don't mind a blood test."

Liz tapped a tablet and a guy in a white lab coat entered. Before anyone could introduce him, Lily held up a glowing hand, enough to make everyone squint. Dang, all of them had left their special light-filtering sunglasses in their gear room. Usually the Anointed could dodge being blinded by her flashes.

"Sorry everyone. There's something different here, so that was brighter than I meant." Lily motioned over to a corner of the control room. "I think our group should chat for a minute. We haven't had a chance since we got here. Oh, and we aren't normally dressed like this." She gestured to her medieval dress and across the rest of them.

Yeah, Demarcus wished for his special running shoes from Ratchet. These boots could cause problems for him.

The Procyon eyes went to Mercury, who glanced around and shrugged. "Don't look at me, I'm not the designated babysitter." When they continued glaring at him, he nodded. "Fine. I guess I brought them in. Yeah, you guys huddle up for a minute. Just don't blind us, okay?"

Demarcus joined his friends in the far part of the room. "Good idea. What's everyone thinking?"

"I'm hungry," Harry whispered. Demarcus could smack him for bringing that up. Super speed came with the need to consume more calories. His stomach began to rumble with the suggestion.

"Focus, Harry. We're apparently in a different dimension with some glitches to our powers. I can't fully turn off the light." Lily shook her hand, and in the shadows he noticed that she had a faint glow to her skin.

Sarah Jane sighed. "I think we have to trust these guys and see this through. It sounds like they've had experience with this kind of thing before, so we don't have much choice. I've also been quietly praying, and I feel like we can trust these people."

That fit Demarcus's vibe. Harry and Lily nodded in agreement. They were learning to trust Sarah Jane's instincts more. "Agreed. Maybe we can ask them about food and go along with what they need. I don't mind getting blood work done because I haven't had any labs since getting my speed. I'm curious if they see anything."

"Just as long as I don't have to test or show my gift," Sarah Jane replied.

"Absolutely," Lily replied, squeezing Sarah Jane's hand. "We won't spill the tea on that." Demarcus knew how she felt about keeping her gift private.

They returned to the Procyon group. "Thanks for that. We're on board with working together to figure out how this happened, and hopefully you guys can help us get back. Uh, before curfew if possible."

"Before curfew?" Mercury whistled a tone. "Liz, you're on that."

Harry elbowed Demarcus. "Oh yeah, traveling dimensions made us hungry. Do you guys have any snacks?"

Finally Mercury smiled. "I just found a DoorDash coupon on my phone. You guys like pizza? Carlito's has the best in any dimension, I'd bet."

He swiped on his phone, but before he could dial, a look of bewilderment came over his face.

"What is it?" Demarcus asked.

"Great. It's the kid," Mercury mumbled.

Chapter Five

Iggy Risner

SOMEWHERE OUTSIDE SAN CAMILLO

This story starts a few days after my little brother Oz accidentally released giant flesh-eating crabs from their containment. Oz felt bad, he did. Especially after those things ate that poor farmer's goats.

But like I said, it was an accident.

By the way, my name is Iggy. You probably know me from my countless adventures in the strange world that is Whispering Pines. A sprawling gated community where a typical suburban life is only an illusion. Strange things happen there all the time. Only the parents in our world seem to be blind to everything.

Were there any adults helping us protect the neighborhood from all those plastic dinosaurs that came to life?

Nope!

Did they help us stop a gang of teenage bullies in the soda pop wars?

Nada!

Did they help save the little kids when we battled a giant snot blob?

Are you kidding me? No.

And what about the time the ice cream hypnotized everyone that ate it?

There were no parents!

So, as you can see, I'm sort of a hero. After all, I'm the one that led us into all these battles. Oz and the others may disagree. But my strategic planning kept us safe and victorious.

I guess now is a good reason to explain why I'm writing this. Well you see, Mom and Dad got this crazy idea we needed to bond more as a family, or some sort of nonsense. So, we decided to take a trip to California. Dad borrowed Grandpa's RV. We packed up and headed out.

Now I know what you're probably thinking. How fun! Right? You couldn't be more wrong. Mom decided we needed to see the Grand Canyon. So Dad being Dad took a detour. That was the first mistake.

Long story short, we ended up in Contigo, Nevada, near Area 51. We never made it to the Grand Canyon. Mom and Dad fought over directions, Oz slept, and I found myself secretly wishing alien abduction was real.

But some great things happened while there. And I documented the entire thing in my new adventure: *Iggy & Oz: The Hairless Sasquatch*. You might want to read that sometime. It's sure to be an award winner with glowing Five Star reviews.

Hopefully they actually send royalties to me instead of the geeky dad in Edmond, Oklahoma. Not sure how that mix-up keeps happening.

Anyway, I'm writing this in a college ruled notebook I found in an old backpack at a deserted rest stop. Both the backpack and the rest stop had seen better days. The pages are slightly water stained but they're blank, and that's all I need.

I woke to the smell of rotting flesh. I sat up, heard the groan of a chainsaw off in the darkness. I wasn't sure if I had taken a blow to the head or what. Everything was a slight fog. After a few minutes I realized the smell was Oz's foot on my face and the chainsaw was only Dad snoring in the back of the RV.

We'd driven most of the day and Dad needed a break. Mom said she did as well, but I think she needed a break from arguing with Dad about how he has no idea where we are or are headed.

What can I say? Parents! They never learn.

I quietly moved to the front of the RV where my tablet was charging on the small table. I snuck a look back. No one moved. I eased the door open and stepped outside. All my life had been built around this moment. I couldn't believe it when Dad said where we were going. A part of me wanted it to be a surprise. But late last night I had emailed Loredana to let her know we were heading to San Camillo. I couldn't believe it. We will be there an entire week.

I needed training from Mercury in order to face the dangers ahead. Loredana had said he would be thrilled to do such a thing for his apprentice, and then encouraged me to call him to let him know we were coming.

I swiped up and hit the call to issue a video chat.

Mercury's face appeared on the screen.

Mercury rubbed his eyes. I knew it. He couldn't believe it. He was pumped to hear from me. I knew there was something special when Loredana told me I was his apprentice.

"Mercury," I said. "Hey! It's Iggy."

"Hey Iggy," Mercury said. "I would love to chat and everything —"

"Oh man, Mercury you're not going to believe this," I said. "But we have been dealing with some major problems."

"Listen, Iggy I really—"

"First Mom and Dad wanted to take a family vacation.

You know, for some bonding or something crazy like that. Of course they fought about where to go. Dad wanted to go northeast to Drake City. Mom wanted to hit the Grand Canyon."

"That's great, Iggy, but I really—"

"But you know, Dad took a wrong turn and we ended up near Area 51 in the town of Contigo. That's when things got crazy. I met a group of teens that know a lot about the stuff happening in our town. You remember Mr. Chesterson? They had a file on him . . ."

"Oh, Mr. Chesterson. Iggy, I hate to—"

"Then Oz released these giant flesh-eating crabs that stand about eight feet tall . . ."

"Cool, giant flesh-eating crabs—"

"That's when Dad said we were heading to San Camillo. I thought that's so cool. So I emailed Loredana and she said you could train me while we were there."

"Yep, San Camillo that sounds . . . Wait? She said what?"

"She said you could train me."

"Who are you talking to?" Two faces appeared behind Mercury. A young black kid with dreadlocks and a redheaded kid.

"Who's that?" I asked.

Mercury moved away. "Just a bunch of kids. Listen, Iggy. It's great you're coming to San Camillo but I —"

"I knew you would be pumped," I said. "Listen, Dad is getting up soon so I need to go. But I'll see you in a few days."

"Wait," Mercury said. "We really need—"

"Oof. Dad's up. Got to run."

I hung up the call and darted back to the RV. Man, this was going to be great. Dad stepped out of the RV. He scrunched up his nose.

"What's that smell?" He asked.

I shrugged. "Smells like crab or lobster." I stopped and spun around. No, they were all captured. Just my mind playing tricks on me.

"Hey Dad," I said. "How much longer until we get to San Camillo?"

"Probably be there in less than an hour," he said. "So long as you Mother lets me handle the directions." Dad glanced over his shoulder then leaned down to whisper. "Might be best if you didn't mention I said that."

I shrugged. "Sure thing, Dad."

"Oh, and we're heading someplace cool. We're going to go visit the Fantastic Fizz Soda Museum."

"Okay," I said. Soda museum. Sometimes Dad comes up with some crazy ideas. But I figured I could handle a few boring minutes at a museum. I stepped into the RV, grabbed my notebook, and started making a list of every-thing I needed to discuss with Mercury. There was so much I needed him to teach me.

Chapter Six

Mercury Hale

I really could've used a vacation at that point. It was bad enough I had four mystery teens hanging out in Tracking, waiting for me to figure out what to do with them, but knowing Iggy Risner was on his way didn't help me feel better about the situation.

Look. He was a nice kid. But he and his brother had a knack for getting into otherworldly trouble. Loredana had pointed Procyon resources in their direction a couple of times without anyone knowing so we could see if we could figure out what was going on.

Plastic toy dinos coming to life and attacking people.

Kids drinking sodas that gave them superpowers.

A pile of snot rampaging through their neighborhood.

And I thought San Camillo had it bad. At least no one had been killed in Iggy's neighborhood—I think.

"Hey, you wanted open communication in our marriage," I told Loredana over the phone.

"I did but I envisioned it as more direct and with less . . . Whinging." She sounded tired but I wasn't about to point that out. I'd heard pregnancy has that side effect. "Don't be so hard on Iggy. He's fairly fond of you, you know."

"Yeah, I know. I've been trying to keep up our communications. Without whinging. Whatever that means."

"Most Americans say 'whining' but they're clearly mispronouncing the word. When he arrives, do take good care of him. The Whispering Pines investigations have borne little fruit. I must say, I'm half-tempted to send in youth of our own. The children in Oklahoma seem far more able to dig up these mysterious occurrences than even our top Intelligence people."

"Bet Cordelia thinks that's great."

"She's rather unamused."

I rubbed at my forehead. "So, these other kids . . ."

"Yes. I cannot say if Procyon has encountered another alternate Earth, albeit one with—how did your text put it? 'Jesus-powers.' I don't think the Scriptures mention X-ray vision, no matter the translation."

"Don't tell Demarcus. He'll give you chapter and verse." I sighed. "So, nothing even in the historic archives?"

"Not that I can discover yet. I have Cordelia digging, of

course, and I'm sure Liz will leave no byte unturned in her analysis."

"Well, she may have Cyril the supercomputer on it but I sent her downstairs to the lab with the kids," I said. "She and Narang were gonna run some blood tests to back up their scans, maybe see how the kids do what they do."

"And the pulsar stave . . ."

I lifted the metal rod. It wasn't much to look at, besides the weathered arcane carvings, when it was unpowered. Still supernaturally cold, though. "Demarcus made it work, no problem. I mean, he wasn't holding his own in a major astral fiend brawl, but it activated for him."

"Yet the tachyon scans were inconclusive."

"Yeah, nothing there."

"Hence the blood tests."

"Yep. Hence." My stomach grumbled. Right. In all the wacky shenanigans I'd kind of forgotten that my lunch had gotten a certain someone's butt prints mashed across it during the fight.

"I am sorry about your pizza."

"You sound way too amused to be sorry."

"Yes, well, I can be both." Loredana grunted.

"You okay?"

"Bloody little beggars." The words were sharp but her tone was more exhausted than anything else. "I would dearly enjoy a day in which every food did not make me want to vomit even as I crave abnormal combinations."

"Are we out of jam again?"

"Yes. To go with the sausages and pickles."

"I'll grab some later. Just stay away from the pepperoni in the back of the fridge."

"Too late, my love."

I closed my eyes and bounced the corner of my phone off my forehead. Could I really smell that sweet, spicy aroma through the cell signal? Nah. Probably just my pants.

One of the techs cleared her throat. "Forecasting for you," she said. "And you'll probably want to know about the tachyon spikes forming uptown."

"Super-duper. Loredana? I've got to go. Probably another emergency. I promise I'll get Ramos to chaperone me this time." I blew a kiss into the phone. What? I'm sappy. "Love you."

"I love you, too."

I was already out of Tracking's door and halfway to the Forecasting office. Of course, I had to stop outside the door and knock three times, but the murmured "Come in," almost didn't happen fast enough.

Forecasting was the soft, carpeted, warmly lit opposite of Tracking. Our resident Forecaster, Edith Pathkiller, was seated cross-legged in the middle of the floor. She'd been kind enough to put out a cushy pillow covered in a hideous argyle pattern. There wasn't any other furniture in the room, except for a chair and desk at the back.

"Hey." I plopped onto the pillow. Kind of forgot about the pizza stains on my pants. "Sorry about—"

"It'll come out." She cracked open one eye. They were a deep, dark brown, but rimmed with glowing purple. The golden light glinted off a tiny wolf nose piercing. She'd draped a ponytail over one shoulder. I knew it was the same place she sported a maroon paw print tattoo but she'd foregone cut-off sleeves for a loose, flowing button-down shirt. The lady liked her flannel, that was for sure, and with the AC cranked up to max. "I can tell you already you won't like what I have to say."

"Do I ever?" I worked out a crick in my neck. "The rips have been forming fast and furious."

She closed her eyes again. Light seeped between her lashes. "The Interstice is unsettled, more than we're used to. I'm sure Tracking has told you that."

I nodded, then remembered her eyes were closed. "Yeah. I've seen the results, too. It's been a heck of a busy summer."

"There's so many possibilities that they show up in my dreams as muddled images. I have one happening soon, though, as far as I can tell."

"Soon? That's not real precise."

Her eyes snapped open. Yikes. I forgot how otherworldly and intimidating they looked when she was in full-on Forecast mode. They had gone white as lightbulbs. "Did I stutter when I used the word muddled? The vision is here."

"Great." I held out my hand. "Standard protocol?"

Edith gave me a wry smile. "Ladies and gentlemen, he can be trained."

"I'm glad you think me getting my brain warped is hysterical."

"Mercury, at the risk of repeating myself, I'll say it again, because beating you over the head with the obvious seems to be the best method of teaching—the future isn't anything to fear. Neither is the past. One hasn't arrived yet. The other is long gone. But the gift of a glimpse of what's to come is the best way to prepare your mind, not warp it."

"I know that. Believe it or not, I have learned something."

"I believe it." Edith's fingers slid across my palm. They were fire hot.

Whatever actually happened—whether I was yanked into the future or experienced an extension of her vision— I felt like the unseen force pulled me from Procyon's towers and whipped me through walls, through clouds, until I thought I was gonna throw up.

Next thing I knew I was in a sprawling atrium. Rainbow walls spread above me and around me. Rainbow . . . glass. An earthquake shook the glass, which curved. They weren't colorful themselves, I realized, but full of sloshing liquid.

Fizzy liquid.

Soda?

The vision snapped me back into the Forecasting room so suddenly I toppled backward off the cushion. Edith was already on her feet, the glow fading from her eyes.

I looked up at her. "Fantastic Fizz Soda Museum."

"It's now." Edith bit the words off. "You've got to *move.*"

"Yeah, I'm going." I pushed to my feet and gestured toward the door. "I could use backup."

Edith's hands trembled. She pressed them together, intertwining her fingers. "I—no. Not yet. It isn't the right time."

Whether she was talking about another vision she'd Forecasted or whether she meant she was still traumatized by her abduction and the brutal battles that had followed wasn't really clear to me but I wasn't about to push her. It hadn't helped matters that she'd had to kill a former operative who Procyon had thought was dead.

The man she'd been deeply in love with.

That last thought cramped up my stomach worse than the vision trip, but I nodded back to her. "I got it. No problem. You've got to take the time you need. We'll be there for you when you're ready."

I headed out into the hallway and took the turn toward the stairs. It'd be a lot faster than waiting for the elevator.

The soda museum? "Perfect," I muttered. "Nothing breakable there."

I remembered to tap my earbud. "Hey, Liz? Hang onto the kids for a while, will you? I've got a rip forming and there isn't time to call in the cavalry."

"Oh! I saw the alert come through from Forecasting. Cyril's confirmed the rip formation and yeah, you don't have a lot of time. Do you need anything else? We've got so many people out on other assignments—"

"Nope, I'm good." I shoved open the exit door and leapt over the railing. My shoes slapped down hard on the next landing. "It's time to suit up."

Chapter Seven

Demarcus Bartlett

Demarcus couldn't hear his stomach rumble over Harry's complaining about being hungry. One minute, Mercury was bragging up some pizza place, then he was answering a phone call and wandered off somewhere in the building. It had been forty-five minutes. Either the pizza place was swamped, slower than his memaw back home, or Mercury had ditched them.

Sarah Jane leaned into their circle in the corner of the Procyon Tracking office. "So we're not getting any food, are we?"

"These guys probably have something they call 'ration packets' that are scientifically modified to taste as awful as possible," Lily groaned.

That's it. If the girls were hungry, they had to do something.

Demarcus zipped over to Liz. He misjudged his speed

and the breeze from his stop blew her pink hair spikes back. "Sorry about that. Is there any food around? Interdimensional travel has made us really hungry."

Liz flipped a tablet over as her eyes darted around. "I think we have some of our special ration bars. They're . . . great." The enthusiasm in her voice drained as she finished that sentence.

Too bad for her that he was able to speed read the tablet and saw the messages about Mercury out on some mission. He also scanned her fancy computer and noted some kind of museum on a map of San Camillo.

"Ration bars sound interesting." Demarcus gave his best spin on it, but wasn't sure he sold the performance. "Can we have some?"

Liz somehow both praised and apologized for the pending food offering, an interesting accomplishment. She scurried off. Then he quickly grabbed the tablet and took in the details he needed. Mercury had ditched them and was off to check out some "rift" at a soda pop museum. Dashing to his friends, they looked up expectantly.

"Pul-eeeze tell me the pizza is coming any moment," Harry whined.

"No, just some ration packets."

Light flared from Lily's hands. "I can't believe it."

Were their powers all acting quirky here? Demarcus just misjudged his speed, and Lily's been softly glowing and spiking flares easily. Harry couldn't teleport right. There had to be some dimensional issue affecting them.

If they only had access to Ratchet and Simon . . .

But regarding Simon, that would never happen.

"There's more. Mercury ditched us. He's off on some mission to check out something called a rift. We're sitting here being babysat when they could use our help."

Sarah Jane motioned for them to lean in close. "Then we go help him. Show them we can help. I think we're in San Camillo for a reason. Who knows why God thinks we should be in another dimension, but we aren't finding answers sitting in a corner."

They all stared at her. "What? Yeah, I'm usually the cautious one, but that's what my spirit is saying. Don't be so shocked."

A strange tingling built up in Demarcus's hands again. The metal sensation of the pulsar stave chilled his skin—except it wasn't in his grip. What had that weapon done?

Lily noticed him looking at his palms. "What is it? Something's going on."

"It's almost like I have the pulsar stave in my hand. So freaky."

Harry put his hand on Demarcus's shoulder and his eyes shot wide, even shadowed by the wizard hat. "Dude, I know where Mercury is. I think I can take us there."

Lily quickly grabbed Demarcus's hand and held her

other out to Sarah Jane. "Should we go?"

Her eyes gleamed. "Oh yeah."

She grasped Lily's hand, completing the connection so that Harry could port them all, just as Liz approached with a box of rations. Demarcus noticed her mouth drop open just as the room around them warped and vanished.

They appeared on grass just outside a glass building with rainbow colors just inside. The lettering over the entrance in a cartoony font read, "Fantastic Fizz Soda Museum."

"Cool, I guess. If we can't get food, at least I can pound down a soda," Harry said.

Then a man in a lightning suit crashed through one of the windows and tumbled across the grass. Mercury groaned and spat.

Demarcus dashed over to help him up. When he reached Mercury, projectiles started flying at him, forcing him to go defensive instead of helping out. He caught one, a can that read "Fierce Cola." That was a brand they didn't have on his Earth.

Sarah Jane called out a warning, and before a bottle could knock him in the head, it shattered from a beam of light. Something like root beer showered him. Now he was stuck in a different dimension, wearing weird clothes, and sticky as a sweet roll.

A rumble came from inside the building, shaking the ground. Mercury stood up, shaking the soda off as best he could. More windows tumbled as a twisted version of a fountain machine skittered out of the museum toward them. Hoses writhed. A nozzle shot a stream of liquid at Lily, knocking her back. "It's like Sprite, and it stings the eyes!" she cried.

Harry ported over to Lily, but he was in the air ten feet above her. He flailed as he fell to the ground, and they both let out a huff of breath when he collided with her.

Demarcus turned to Mercury. "This kind of thing happens often around here, I guess? How do we take it out?"

Mercury flicked his wrist, and the pulsar stave flashed to life. "How about you get its attention and I'll do what I do best. Slay monsters."

He wasn't sure about being a distraction, but Demarcus hadn't battled anything like this, and Mercury seemed to know his stuff when they first met at the park. "On it," he said before dashing around the side of the fountain machine from hell. What do you even call this thing, anyway?

Carbonated water blasts chased him, but the monster couldn't anticipate where he was going fast enough to hit him—until it sprayed some purple mist ahead of him on a sidewalk. Demarcus's stupid boots had minimal traction, and he slipped and tumbled all the way until he smacked a glass wall. Shards of glass scraped his shirt, drawing blood, and his head throbbed with the impact.

At least his feint worked, because Mercury was flying through the air ready to impale the stupid soda beast. Then his body jerked and he tumbled to the side of the fiend. A walking, snarling vending machine shot cans of fizzy death at Mercury, who furiously spun the stave to keep from getting concussed.

Demarcus saw a power cord trailing this new threat, so he shook his arms and took off to pull the power. He bent down and yanked the cord out of the socket, but nothing happened. The vending monster's cord wrapped around his arm and wrenched him hard to the ground. He was whipped around on the cement to the front of the machine, where the door to get the can out grew teeth that started chomping, dragging Demarcus closer to the maw.

Man, only a chump would go out to a freaky soda machine.

Chapter Eight

Iggy Risner

If there is one thing I have hoped to avoid as a kid, it's the Cheetos fingers. But no matter what one does, it can't be avoided. Right now the AC is out in the RV. Mom says it's Dad's fault. Not sure how, but his face is about five shades of red which means he probably is quietly agreeing.

Dad quietly agrees with Mom a lot.

Anyway, Oz got the munchies and found a bag of Cheetos. I'm trying hard not to barf, but he keeps dipping his sweaty hands into the bag, and well, his fingers are orange and now so is his white Area 51 shirt Mom just bought him. Man, he's going to be toast when she sees him.

It's tough being the mature one. I love my family. But sometimes they embarrass me so much I find myself re-evaluating my entire childhood.

Now look, I don't want to be a downer, but in terms of quality San Camillo seems kind of worn down. I'm not sure what I expected. Maybe I thought I would come across folks in cloaks walking the streets with staves in hand, or possibly see a few random rips for one to travel through. Maybe even come across a rogue astral fiend chilling in the park. But nope, it was just a typical town. A few boarded-up stores on Main Street, some unkept yards, and a Volkswagen missing wheels and sitting on some cinder blocks. Mom told Dad we took a wrong turn and ended up on the wrong side of the tracks. I'm not sure what she meant, but this makes the Procyon Foundation seem even less climatic.

I might need to chat with Mercury about moving their base of operation to Whispering Pines. It would certainly be easier on my training and our little neighborhood was full of far more excitement.

We rounded the corner and headed down a long curvy road. At the end was a tall glass building with some wild rainbow colors inside.

"This is it!" Dad said.

"Whoa! What is this place?" Oz asked.

"Fantastic Fizz Soda Museum. Looks a little childish," I said. I didn't have time for this nonsense. I needed to find Mercury. I needed to start my training. I glanced at the tablet. Still no messages from him. Okay, just get through this little tour, and then find a way to plan a meet up. Maybe I could convince Mercury to give Mom and Dad a tour of the foundation's facility. Something to keep them busy.

Dad brought the RV to a park in the middle of an empty parking lot. I glanced out the window. The place looked like a ghost town.

"Are you sure they're open?" My Mom asked. "They look closed."

"I know," Dad said. "I don't get it. Chesterson told me they were always open. Twenty-four seven and even on the holidays."

I perked up and looked at Dad. "Mr. Chesterson told you about this place?"

Dad turned around and laughed. "What is it with you and that man, Iggy? But yes, he told me about it three or four weeks before he passed. Said he used to run the place. That man had a fascination with soda."

Oz tapped me on the shoulder. "Iggy, remember the soda pop machine? What if—"

"I know, Oz. I remember. Let me try and piece it all together. Mr. Chesterson used to manage the Fantastic Fizz in the same town as the Procyon Foundation. Oz, you know what this means?"

Oz shrugged and licked his fingers. "That people like soda pop here?"

I rolled my eyes. Explaining complex theories was difficult. "Oz, you just brought up the soda pop machine that came from Mr. Chesterson's house. Clearly you know what I'm talking about."

"I was just curious if they have any of that strawberry wind soda you drank that one time." Oz doubled over laughing. "Oh, man. Remember that one, Iggy? Wow that stunk."

How could I forget? I had once drunk soda that gave me the power to pass gas so lethal that it knocked people out. In the world of superpowers, it wasn't ideal. Especially when the girl of your dreams is standing right there.

Another thing I plan to have Mercury teach me about. How to impress girls!

We hopped out of the car and headed inside. Dad seemed to be ecstatic. Not sure why. To Dad it was just a soda museum. To me and Oz, knowing Mr. Chesterson had once been here deepened the mystery of the man even more. Not to mention gave me caution as to what this place possibly was. See, we kids have a responsibility to protect our parents from the deep mysteries of the world. So, this is sort of top secret. No way Mom and Dad could handle the truth Oz and I know. As much as it pained me, letting Dad just see it as a soda museum was for the best.

The door to the museum was unlocked. We strolled in. I couldn't let the family know, but man, was it impressive. Hundreds, no, let's make that thousands of sodas lined the walls on shelves that climbed at least thirty feet up on three different floors. This would be a kindergartner's dream! Well, and Dad's.

"Check these out," Dad said. He grabbed a soda that was clear and read the label. "Lemon Lime Nap."

"This one says Strawberry Wind," Mom said, reading the label on a red colored soda.

I quickly glanced up. "Um, I've had that Mom, trust me it's not that great."

"It doesn't taste bad!" Mom said.

"Ugh, Iggy," Oz said. "Did she just . . ."

FRAAAP BRAAAP

Look, there is no way to write this. It sounded like the Hindenburg exploding. Maybe the Titanic slamming against an iceberg. Oh forget it, think of a thousand cows ripping one at once and you got it.

I covered my face in time and put my head between my legs.

"My eyes, Iggy!" Oz screamed. "It's burning my eyes."

I grabbed Oz by the hand and sprinted to the other side of the room. When I looked back Mom and Dad were both sitting in chairs, passed out. The empty bottle of soda rolled across the floor towards us. I picked it up and read the label.

Strawberry Wind: Extra Strength

Oh, lovely.

"Iggy," Oz said. "What do we do?"

I shook my head. "I'm not sure, but I don't think they're getting up anytime soon."

"Iggy, I need some air. I'm choking on this."

I grabbed and pushed him toward the door. I had to agree. I'm not sure what Mom ate, but she had something growing in her for sure. It was right as we were heading outside I heard the noises. It sounded like an explosion. As we pushed the door open I saw him, my mentor Mercury. He wasn't alone, though.

"Is that a soda machine attacking that kid?" Oz asked.

"I'm not sure," I said. "But come on, they need our help."

I sprinted toward the kid with dreadlocks. At the moment he was fighting a power cord that was wrapping more and more around his neck. I'm not sure the kid had ever fought the supernatural before, but he had potential.

I figured it was time for me to step in.

Chapter Nine

Mercury Hale

I'd love to say things were going great. I really would. Except that would be lying and that's not a great thing to do, especially not around children.

My head felt like someone had taken an ice bucket, slammed the lid shut, and shaken it a couple of dozen times so they could whip up the perfect cocktail for James Bond. No, I don't think he ever took ice. See what I mean? Brains sufficiently rattled to mess up simple movie lore.

I was supposed to be the hero. I was supposed to be in charge. But there I was, sprawled flat on the lawn—again— wondering how I was gonna get the grass unstuck from the multiple layers clinging to my suit while a bunch of kids battled it out with a mutated vending machine beast that was way tougher than it looked.

"Battled it out" might be a generous description. The thing was dragging Demarcus toward a tooth-filled maw just like an astral fiend's, except more metal and machine than slobbering natural fang. Nothing about the way it looked changed the fact that the kid would be dead.

I would have taken care of it myself but I was busy deflecting soda can missiles. Sounds ridiculous, right? It felt a lot more painful than ridiculous, because the soda machine launcher monster was just as powerful as an astral fiend and he was flinging fizzy projectiles my way as quickly as grenades launched by the San Camillo PD's task force guys in their body armor.

"Hang on!" Harry vanished, then reappeared twelve feet past Demarcus. Pretty slick teleport move, even if the kid had miscalculated his arrival—or maybe it was a glitch like he'd mentioned before. In any case, I think Dominic Zein would have been proud, except the first monster—the one created from a massively overgrown, nightmare version of a soda foundation—blasted him with a spray of clear and pink soda that was less of a spray and more of a deluge from a breached dam.

That blast didn't do me any good, because it kept me from Demarcus, but it turned out I wasn't the only one with a plan. A soda can hurtled through the air, spinning end over end. It exploded with such force you could see the shockwave outlined in fizzy bubbles.

"Hey! Leave him alone, metal head!"

The voice was way too high-pitched to come from the

teenagers. Just what I was worried about—the kid. Iggy Risner.

I was still kind of floored that he was here in my city. Even more floored that he'd shown up in the midst of our fight among the soda museum. But there he was, standing with his legs spread and his face bent into a scowl like he was ready to trade fists with somebody twice his size.

He wasn't using his fists, though. He reached behind without looking. His little brother, Oz, picked up another can of soda from the ground and handed it to him. The cans were bright green, and I mean *bright*, like a night-club's pulsating sign. I glimpsed the words "Neon Nuke" in shimmering yellow letters before Iggy shook the can with both hands and then let it fly.

The next explosion actually made me stagger a bit. The monster shrieked and backed away. Its power cord loosened. Better yet, the back-to-back soda bombs distracted the other monster, the one pelting us with its own soda ammo, enough that I could reach out with half of the pulsar stave and let it have a concentrated blast of extradimensional energies right in its metal and plastic face.

Blinding light bathed the entire scene. I had to hand it to Lily: being able to act like a human spotlight made for a great way to stop a monster from trying to kill us, but the downside was we hadn't fought on the same team long enough for me to remember to squint.

Even more impressive was, as I blinked away the purple spots, she clobbered the monster machine with a rippling wave of light or energy or plasma from her hands. Liz must have been salivating over the readouts from whatever drone she had monitoring the place.

I dragged Demarcus upright. "You okay?"

"Yeah, man. Rattled." He had a couple of bruises on his face and his knuckles were scraped, but otherwise he looked intact.

"Mercury!" Iggy grinned up at me. "Hi."

"Hey, kid." I couldn't help grinning back at him, but felt a bit awkward. How was I supposed to act around kids? I ruffled his hair with a free hand. "Good job."

Oz snorted. "He thinks you're a dog," he stage-whispered to his brother.

"No, he *doesn't*," Iggy hissed. "So, um, Mercury . . . What's our plan?"

"Our plan?" I shook my head. "Sorry, Iggy. This isn't the part where we join forces in an epic team-up. This is the real world. In the real world, I've got to keep teenagers from getting killed by the monsters trying to tear apart the soda museum."

"We're doin' just fine on our own." Demarcus crouched for a second, like he was getting ready for a marathon, then disappeared in a gust of wind and a blur of smeared colors.

Oz jumped a half foot in the air. "Woah! Did he tele-port?"

"Nope. That's Harry's deal." Speaking of the devil. Harry blinked back into existence behind one of the soda machine beasts, with Lily alongside him, her arm looped through his. They could have been going to prom—a medieval prom since they were still dressed like Renaissance fair nerds.

"Mercury!" Lily raised her hands. "When I get him . . ."

"Hey, ugly!" Harry kicked the soda machine monster right in its steely posterior.

It spun toward them and split down the middle, jagged metal and glass forming mangled teeth. The power cord whipped around like a scorpion's tail.

Lily's light slammed full force into the monster's so-called face.

The critter writhed. It slipped on its own soda, and trust me, there was enough of it that it had a heck of a time finding solid footing.

"Stay back, Iggy!" I advanced on the beast, pulsar staves humming in either hand, both scattering lightning sparks along the ground.

Lily's blasts hadn't done the trick. But I knew what would.

Demarcus swept in, appearing almost as suddenly as Harry had, except you could actually see him skidding to a stop, and he wasn't alone. He was pushing a soda dispenser not unlike the one that had sprayed me and sent it careening into its twin. They crashed against a wall, crumpling tiles.

My boots squelched through sticky soda as I pivoted, leveled the staves, and blasted gaping holes through both the dispensers. They slumped onto the floor, steam rising from the jagged gashes as the edges cooled from red-hot.

"He's coming back around!" Harry shouted.

Right. The monster Lily had blinded. It had resorted to flailing with its power cord—make that *four* cords—but kind of had some aiming problems. Which was good for me and the rest of the gang.

That didn't stop it from whipping towards Lily.

Harry dove in front of her, arms spread, probably ready to yoink them both out of there in another awesome teleporting move, except he stood there like a kid in a high school play who'd forgotten his lines. His expression morphed in about two seconds from confusion to fear.

A monstrous power cord bashed against his forehead. Harry dropped into Lily's arms. She sagged against his weight until she was on her knees.

Something grabbed my ankles and slammed me onto the ground, too. More cord tentacles. And they'd grown glass-shard spikes, which felt great where they dug into my skin, sarcasm intended.

I cut through them with the pulsar stave and lunged toward the last monster. It had itself wrapped around Harry and didn't seem to care that Lily was screaming, in tears, as light streamed from one outstretched hand.

More soda cans went hurtling through the air, and not just the one or two at a time Iggy had lobbed before. Demarcus was spinning them one after the other in an endless stream from a pile heaped at his feet.

"Get him more! Get him more!" Oz raced up to Demarcus with another armload. Great idea. Until he dropped one and it exploded at his feet. Oz wound up on his butt, expression dazed.

I shoved off the ground and ducked beneath Demarcus's barrage of Neon Nukes. The flashing colors and bubbling shockwaves created a miniature stormfront in the museum, which made for great cover, but the monster still wouldn't back off of Harry's limp form.

That was okay. I was happy it was a frozen target.

I pieced the pulsar stave back together and drove it deep into the crevice where the machine monster had split itself down the middle.

That did the trick.

The monster exploded in a hail of pulverized metal, smoldering plastic, and freezing chunks of glass. The soaking soda spray didn't make the impact from that hailstorm any softer, that's for sure.

No chunky residue left behind like an astral fiend. Not a bit remaining. Just like the mutated jungle gym at Century Park.

"Well." I swiped the sticky residue off my mask's eyepiece. I wondered if Liz could install mini wiper blades. "That was awful."

And I wasn't just talking about us taking a beating. The soda museum's first floor was a wreck. We had to have demolished a good half of it, right up to and including the gift shop. I mean, look, the bulk of the damage was due to the ugly monster triplets, but they weren't around to dodge police inquiries or pay bills.

"Really hope Procyon didn't skimp on its contingency fund this month," I muttered.

Iggy whooped. He gave Demarcus a high five. "We did it!"

Demarcus seemed less than enthused. He was already storming away from Iggy and Oz, with a bit of a limp, I noticed. "Sarah Jane, where is he?"

The redheaded girl. What was her role on their team, anyway? It had just occurred to me she didn't run fast, teleport, or blast light beams. She had her hands on Lily's shoulders as Lily did her best to sit upright. Harry was gone.

"Where's Harry?" I'm a master at blurting the obvious.

"I-I don't know." Sarah Jane lowered her gaze. "He was

right here, injured by that, that thing, but by the time I reached Lily he'd gone."

"Demarcus." Lily's voice shook. "It looked like he teleported."

"While he was knocked out?" Demarcus ran his hands over his dreads. "Oh, man. Is that even a thing he can do? Like a reflex?"

"I don't know. But he'd been having trouble with his ability . . ." Lily took Sarah's hands. Together they closed their eyes. I caught a few of Lily's murmured words as I got closer. A few sounded suspiciously like "Lord." They were right. No sign of Harry. Just a limp cable with a leftover lopsided loop where it had ensnared his leg.

That, of course, was when San Camillo's finest burst onto the scene. Twelve men and women in uniform, complete with Kevlar vests. Lieutenant Gabriel Ramos was front and center, naturally. He stepped gingerly around the biggest pool of soda, as if afraid it was going to ruin his Oxford wingtips, which it probably would. Ramos lifted his mirrored sunglasses.

"Mercury." Talk about getting a stern talking-to in peak Dad-voice. "What have you done now?"

I glanced down at Iggy and Oz, who must have decided the safest place was huddled next to the superhero and not the incriminating Neon Nukes. "You see, guys? Zero trust."

Chapter Ten

Mercury Hale

I stood staring up at the floors stocked with endless rainbow rows of soda. Every color you can imagine. The sight would make the manufacturers of Skittles jealous.

Way too many of those bottles were broken.

"That's . . . impressive." Ramos removed his sunglasses. I hadn't heard him approach. If Loredana and I ever got a cat, we'd have to name it Ramos, or Gabriel, or Lieutenant Fluffy von Pawprints. The guy could sneak up on *anyone.*

I glanced at him. "You thinking what I'm thinking?"

"Yes." He then said, "Tens of thousands of dollars in property damage" at the same time I blurted "Who has Mentos?"

Ramos sighed. "I regret asking already, but here I go: what were you thinking?"

"I can explain." I waved my arm at the ruined floors,

the broken windows, and the endless sticky puddles of spilled soda. "Things in here came to life. These kids from another dimension used their superpowers to help me fight the machinery that's been affected by the same odd dimensional breach that turned the jungle gym at Century Park into a metal version of an astral fiend."

"That's . . . Ah." Ramos plucked his notebook from a pocket and started scribbling notes with his pen. "Given everything else we've been through, that isn't the strangest explanation I've encountered."

"Like when we had the guy with ice powers and his werewolf buddy help us destroy the fiery mutant fiend."

"I think the friend was actually a human-fox hybrid."

"No need to nitpick." He was right, of course. I sniffed at my sleeve. The super suit was going to need serious laundering. "Look, I need to go check on them and get back to Procyon. They're pretty upset about their friend disappearing."

"As I would imagine they should be." Ramos's pen scratched notes. "Do you have any word from Liz as to what's causing these new kinds of creatures to appear?"

I shook my head. "Nothing yet. She's got some theories about weirder-than-usual tachyon spikes but when it comes to concrete answers we're a bit short right now."

"When was the last time you had rips open up without astral fiends appearing?"

"Besides Cavill Cemetery?" I shrugged. "Not even sure that one counted as a rip. Plus, we haven't actually confirmed that's what happened in these cases. Look, when I know, you'll know, okay?"

"All right." Ramos watched me intently, like he was expecting me to teleport. News flash. Not one of my tricks. "Are you okay?"

"Me? Sure. Fine." I shook my head. "Why wouldn't I be fine trying to figure out how to get a group of teenagers back to their home dimension, while losing one of them in the process?"

"You're worried about them."

"Gold star for you. Yes, Ramos, I'm worried about them. They're my responsibility. The four of them are on their own in a strange world, without anyone looking out for their well-being, so I'm not gonna sit back and hope things work out for the best. I'll stop whatever these new monsters are and I'll make sure they get back home safely."

Ramos smiled. He slid his sunglasses back on.

"What?"

"Nothing."

"That's not a 'nothing.' You're smiling. You're the guy who saves smiles for special occasions, like birthdays or your wife's anniversary or when you're about to say 'I told you so.' Right?"

"Let's say I think you're learning what you should learn and leave it at that. Tell your Manager Alvarez I'll have this cleaned up, but if you want to avoid the press, you'd better head out a back door with the rest of your Procyon people."

Ramos wasn't kidding. SCPD had six officers holding a pack of local reporters at arm's length. I wasn't up for interviews.

And I was pretty sure Alvarez wasn't keen on more publicity. Call it a hunch. Or maybe it was what he said to me after the Echelon Plaza incident—*"So help me Mercury, if we get any more publicity, I will make you an actual janitor instead of just being one on paper to disguise what you really do."*

Yeah. Great boss.

When I walked back into the Tracking office, toweling off my hair from the 30-second shower I'd taken—in lukewarm water, thanks very much—everybody was talking at the same time.

"You gotta know where he went!" Demarcus was standing right in front of Liz. His arms were spread. "What's all this tech for if you don't?"

"It's my fault." Lily had a hand pressed to the side of her head. She was grimacing and looked too pale. "I had him right there with me."

"No, it's not your fault." Sarah Jane frowned at her. "Are you sure you're okay? You took a couple of bad hits. Lily, he's okay. I know Harry. He'll figure this out."

"Especially if these guys can't." Demarcus glowered at Liz. "Where is he?"

I put my fingers in my mouth and whistled. Never tried that before—but it worked. Everyone turned around. Even Liz spun in her chair. She yelped and clapped her hand down the top of her mug's lid before she sloshed its contents onto the floor.

"Three things." I counted off with my fingers. "One: Everybody settle down and be quiet. Two: Liz, that had better not be soda."

She slowly set the mug on the narrow desk next to her console, then slid it six inches away for good measure.

"And three—"

"That was technically already three, man." Demarcus smirked. "Settle down. Be quiet. No soda."

"*Three*." I glared at him. "Thanks for using all the hot water in the staff bunks."

"You're welcome." Demarcus folded his arms.

What would Ramos say? Probably "Lord give me strength." Well, that actually sounded more like Wilhelmina. I made eye contact with the kids. They had obviously showered, being even more scrubbed up than I was, and had changed into dark gray Procyon T-shirts and navy-blue sweatpants. "Look. We're gonna get your friend back. I promise you. We've got the resources to do it and we've solved bigger problems than this. Right, Liz?"

"Hmm?" She had turned back to her screen, which was filled with so many charts and graphs I had flashbacks to a grueling calculus test. "Yes. Definitely. Uh-huh."

"Okay. Great." I leaned against her desk. "So . . . What's the deal with these rips, and where did the kid go?"

"So, um, the rips." Liz tapped in a couple of commands. Two red diamonds appeared on the big map of San Camillo. "I had Cyril run comparisons between the tachyon spikes these coincided with and others we've experienced and nothing matched until I had him expand the timeline."

"How far back?"

"Forty years." She touched her screen again. Eleven, twelve, thirteen more blips appeared.

I straightened up. "When were these?"

"Between 1979 and 1981. The technology we use for monitoring tachyon spikes that herald a rip opening is pretty new, but they had some rudimentary stuff based on experimental units developed in the late 1960s. It was wonky until the 1990s."

"So, can we even trust these readings?"

"Um, I think so. Yes. Pretty sure. Because when you dig

into the detailed analyses you can see that they don't originate in the Interstice. I think that's why we haven't seen any full-fledged astral fiends and why it's been inanimate objects coming to life, because what's happening is there's another breach that's I guess poking holes between the dimensions and breaking down the—"

"Liz." I pinched my forefinger and thumb together. "Shorter."

"Oh. Right. Um." Liz swiped her fingers across her tablet one more time. "I think it's coming from here."

Threads of red light shot out from the fifteen diamonds and intersected far outside San Camillo's east side, in the forest encircling Arbor Valley. Liz reoriented the map for a bird's-eye view of the landscape that was still crispy from the fiery mutant fiend that had torched the area a few years back, but there was one untouched section that was so thick with over- and under-growth that I had to squint at the rough white rectangle poking from between the canopy. It looked like there might even be a long, but narrow, winding road to it. "What's that?"

"That's the problem, Mercury. The data I have is linked to something called Site 17 but there's nothing in the records about what Site 17 is." Liz chewed her lip. "I mean, I guess there could be something off the database in the Historic Vaults."

Which meant someone was going to have to dig

through musty papers. "And the kid?"

"I'm . . ." Liz glanced at the kids, who were huddled together, gazes glued to the screen. "I'm having trouble," she whispered. "It's possible he went into the Interstice. But I can't tell for sure. His tracker is giving off weird readings."

"Tracker?" I lowered my voice to match her. "Liz, did you lo-jack these kids?"

"Maybe? Yes." She blushed. "It seemed like something Ms. Lark would do."

I grinned. "Best idea you've had so far. You'd better call up Dominic and tell him he's needed for his favorite kind of road trip."

Chapter Eleven

Harry Wales

The dream wouldn't stop. Harry dove in the water to save his friends. Sometimes it was Demarcus or Lily, but most of the time it was Sarah Jane. Every time they disappeared, and he struggled to reach the surface again, bubbles flowing all around him. And when he was about to take his last breath, he appeared at the surface, seeing a friend in need again.

If I could just teleport properly and save them . . .

A flash of light appeared and his eyes slowly opened. Why is Lily going so bright? "Hey Lily, take it down a few notches, okay?" He put his hand over his face and a sweet scent greeted him. He licked his finger. Root beer?

Oh yeah. His friends had joined Mercury Hale, the dude with the awesome lightsaber stick, and were fighting monster versions of soda machines and fountain drink dispensers. The smell sure beat messing around in the mud on Mount Sutro or Hyde Park Pier's fishy odor. Even if his hands were sticky.

The light didn't fade, but his eyes slowly acclimated. Well, mostly. The brightness reminded him of a sunny day in Montana when the ground was covered in snow and the reflection made it hard to see without sunglasses. "Lily, are you there?"

Groaning, he felt a bump on his head that did not like being touched. The front of his robe was torn, and a wicked red streak also hurt when he ran his hand over it. He looked around, but didn't see his friends. Or Mercury. Or anything that looked like civilization.

Where was he now?

Instead of the glass front of the Fantastic Fizz Soda Museum, the landscape was . . . out of focus. Vague outlines of trees, buildings, and rock formations sprawled before him, but try as he might, he couldn't see any definition. Harry took a few steps in a circle, taking in everything. Was this just a concussion?

Wait. There were more flashes. He thought he could make out the silhouettes of Lily's glow and Demarcus's blur. A featureless person with streaks of lightning and a shiny staff. Mercury?

Something about this dimension was futzing with everyone's powers. That must be it. Harry just was off a frequency. Harmonics? Multiversal madness? Something science-y. Now that he could see them, at least he could port there in a—

He disappeared from his position, but landed in a splash of water. Coughing, he stood up and tripped again over some long, gangly roots. Some kind of mangrove tree. *Now what has happened?*

Harry spun around, his heart rate beginning to speed up. This place had focus, but it was a serene and vast area of not much. The ankle-deep water sloshed gently over his robe. A faint ball of light was visible far off on the horizon, too far for him to attempt porting to with his gift so glitchy. There was no sign of his friends' silhouettes.

This was a fine pickle to be in. Oh, why did I have to think of pickles? I'm starving.

He thought back to when he started using the gift. Usually he'd end up in a random spot, like up in a tree or in the middle of a busy intersection where Demarcus had rescued him. Once he learned to do it on his command, it took practice to go farther.

I'll just do a short jump this time.

The air around him warped and he found himself on a steep shard of a rock, sliding down towards the ground as an unnatural storm raged around him. Dude, this was not the place he wanted to be. Before he crashed in the dirt he tried another port and ended up in the blurry space again.

His chest tightened. Invisible bands constricted his

lungs, making every breath labored. Where was he? And how was he going to get out of here?

Before he tripped into a full-blown panic attack, a thought flickered inside him. *When your powers first started, you didn't know Jesus. He's still Lord, even if it's in another dimension. Even another, another dimension.*

Harry began to pray in hushed tones—why he didn't know since there was no one around. He didn't know exactly how to pray about this particular situation, but he poured out words as best he could. His pulse slowed and breathing relaxed. Even if he'd gotten himself in a bigger mess than ever before, he found solace in knowing who he could turn to.

As his words and turmoil quieted, a voice carried softly through the atmosphere. "Is someone there?"

Harry startled so hard he almost ported out of reflex. However, he managed to stay grounded and searched for the source of the words. After a few minutes of scanning, a different type of feature oscillated out of sync with the rest of the fuzzy landscape around him.

Okay, don't teleport and lose this guy. We'll do it the slow way, one step at a time.

Chapter Twelve

Iggy Risner

Wowzers! Man, has this been a wild ride today. Just think, this morning, I was just waking up from the sound of Oz snoring in his sleep, followed by a few toots from Dad. Never, in all of my life, did I imagine I would be on my way to the Procyon Foundation headquarters.

We were being driven in a black SUV by a man named Garvey. He had threatened to turn the car around three times already if Oz didn't sit back and pipe it.

For a dude that told Mercury he could handle the transport because he had three kids, he was performing rather poorly. I intended to inform Mercury of the fellow's insubordination as soon as we arrived at headquarters.

"Mr. Garvey," I said.

The man sighed heavily. "What?"

"I was just curious about how much further until we arrived?"

A large black glass rose between him and us, cutting us off.

"You think it's soundproof?" Oz asked, tapping the glass.

"Of course, it's soundproof," I said. "He probably doesn't have clearance to hear anything we're discussing."

I hated to admit it, but I could see how much Mercury valued me. He gave us a private limo with our own dedicated chauffeur. It was apparent that I was considered significant.

We slowed to a crawl and pulled up next to a cinder block security house. Garvey waved a badge, and the gate slid open.

"What are they mad about?" Oz asked. I glanced out the window and saw several signs that said: "The Truth should be heard by all!!!" "Stop the Lies!!!" It was a mixture of old and young folks.

"Is that guy wearing a tin foil hat?" Oz asked.

"He's trying to keep out the gamma rays from reading his mind," I said.

"Whoa," Oz said. "Do you think they might be reading my thoughts?"

"Nah," I said. I didn't have the heart to tell the kid his thoughts were too chaotic to read.

We pulled to a stop, and Garvey grumpily opened the door. I handed him a two-dollar bill I had kept wadded in my shoe just in case I needed it. It was a little sweaty, but I figured he would overlook it. Instead, he just stared at it and grumbled before walking off. The guy might need to find a new line of work.

I rubbed the gooseflesh forming on my arms. I couldn't believe I was there. The Procyon Foundation headquarters. In front of me were three large towers with glass running up five, six, no at least seven stories.

"Oz," I said. "We're here."

Oz shrugged and glanced over at the black van pulling in. "You think Mom and Dad are okay?"

"I think they'll be out awhile," I said. "That was extra strength Strawberry Wind, and man, did Mom let one rip."

Two men pulled Mom and Dad out of the black van on gurneys and started wheeling them toward the second building.

"Let's go, you two rugrats," Garvey snapped. "I'm supposed to get you upstairs quick."

"They'll be fine," I said. "Come on, let's follow grumps here."

We headed into the third building and followed Garvey to the elevator, where he pressed the button for the seventh floor.

"So," I asked. "How long have you been a chauffeur for Mercury?"

"A chauffeur?" Garvey asked. "Look, kid. I'm a lot more

than a driver. And Mercury . . ."

"I just assumed you had to be pretty experienced to be trusted with driving us."

"Driving you?" He laughed. "I don't even know who you are, and honestly, I'm done answering questions. So let's ride in peace, please."

Oz elbowed me and whispered rather loudly, "I don't think he likes us."

I shrugged. "Who do you think those other kids were?"

"No, idea," Oz said. "But that kid with dreads had super-speed. Did you see how fast he moved?"

"Him?" I said. "Man, did you see that red-headed kid? He teleported here, and then there, and then back here. It was super cool."

"What kind of soda do you think they drank?"

"No idea, but I plan to find out."

"Where did that red-headed kid go?" Oz asked.

I shrugged. "Probably a top-secret Mercury mission. I plan to get one soon, too."

Beside us, Garvey sighed heavily.

"Hey, Mr. Garvey," Oz asked. "Do you have any good dad jokes?"

Garvey sighed again.

"I asked my dad for his best dad joke," Oz said. "He said, 'You!' He's pretty bad at jokes because I didn't get it."

The elevator doors opened, and Oz and I hopped out.

"Oh, look!" A shriek from the other side of the room said. "It's kids. Just like Mercury said!"

The girl bounced over. "How are we?"

"All yours," Garvey said, and quickly disappeared.

"I'm Iggy, and this is my brother Oz. And that guy is a little grumpy."

She laughed. "I'm Liz, and don't mind him. Come with me. I've been instructed to take you to the Historic Vault. We've been looking for some info on Site 17."

"The Historic Vault?" I said. "We get to go to the Historic Vault?"

"Why yes," she said. "And don't worry about your parents. They are in the infirmary with Dr. Arne. We've been studying the soda at the museum. It's quite intriguing."

"Our neighbor used to manage it," Oz said. "He died, though, and everything that came out of his house is cursed and causing all sorts of strange things to happen."

"Oh, yes," Liz said. "I know all about Mr. Chesterson and the tachyon spikes happening in Whispering Pines. Especially after Mercury made his visit."

"Really?" Oz asked. "You know about Mr. Chesterson? How?"

"Well, Cyril has given—"

"Wait!" I brought us to a halt. "You mean Cyril is here?"

"Why yes," Liz said. "Why?"

"He is sort of a super fan," Oz said. "He hopes to join

the Procyon Foundation someday."

Liz laughed. "Oh boy, what has Mercury done? Come, we need to hurry."

I couldn't believe this was all happening. The Historic Vaults! Cyril! My dreams were coming true.

Chapter Thirteen

Mercury Hale

I checked my phone for the fifth time in as many minutes. Funnily enough, me glaring at it didn't make a text from Dominic materialize.

Forget the reply. What I really needed was for him to materialize, sooner rather than later.

Where was everyone, anyway? I'd gone outside to check the perimeter—discreetly, of course. Found Garvey grumbling about "wackos" and "rugrats," shaking his head as he and a couple of his security pals, including Anthony Moses, scowled at the lines of picketers outside the property fence line.

"Isn't it about time they get a new conspiracy theory?" Garvey grumbled. "My triplets are better behaved."

Anthony snorted at the word "time." It was a funny habit he'd picked up over the summer when he was temporarily transferred to the new Patchwork base Procyon had

83

finished fixing up after Syndax's prior attack. "Hey, man, if you were them hearing rumors of the crazy stuff that went on here, wouldn't you be hollering for answers? Especially when you think about the monsters they've seen. And then there's Serena Cyr's videos circulating online—"

"Yeah, okay, it's a mess." I ran my hands through my hair. "Hey Garvey, where'd the kids wind up?"

He gave me one of those looks, the kind I figured he gave his three boys when they asked him why they had to clean their rooms. "Aren't they with Ms. Stojan?"

Ah. Right. I nodded. "Sure. Thanks for that."

Garvey and Anthony glanced at each other but didn't say what they were thinking, which was great, because I was sure it was something like, "I wonder when Mrs. Lark-Hale is getting back?"

I was on my way back through the lobby and headed for the stairwell—because skipping the elevator meant I had time to think and I never gave up the chance to stretch my legs—when I heard giggling from downstairs.

Giggling? From the basement?

The Historic Vault.

The massive, armored vault door was open. Allison glanced up from the desk set to one side. She'd swapped out her retro glasses frames for a brilliant red pair. Short and slim, with blonde hair cut shoulder length, she usually smiled. Except then.

"Oh. Mr. Hale." She glanced over her shoulder. If she had a pencil on her desk to chew, she would have. Instead her frown deepened. "I know it's irregular and trust me, I wouldn't have let Ms. Stojan bring them in if Mrs. Lark-Hale hadn't cleared their access with me personally but—"

I held up my hands. "Allison, the less I know, the better, okay? We're just gonna make sure Alvarez doesn't hear about this before we're both working backup for self-checkout machines at a big box store."

That got me a smile. "You've read my mind. The security feeds are blanked. Courtesy of Ms. Stojan. And my logbook is empty."

"You're the best." I kept a grin on my face but hurried into the Vault really hoping and maybe even praying Liz hadn't made an awful mistake.

There were boxes strewn all over the floor.

I leaned against a set of metal shelves so I didn't pass out. "Liz?"

Her head popped around a corner. There was a bright yellow pen between her teeth. Her eyebrows shot up so fast I thought they'd physically separate from her head. "Oh! Hey! This is great! The boys have such an eye for detail we really should consider having them parse some of the older documents down here for gaps in our data because at the rate they're reading we could find so many answers to anomalies that we could tell the manager—"

"Cool. Really great." I pictured Alvarez staring, mouth wide open, at two kids wearing miniature suits and bearing Procyon ID badges. "Mind telling me why the Historic Vault's got more cardboard boxes littering the floor than my apartment on moving day?"

"Oh. Um. We got a little carried away." She blushed. "There were so many references to Site 17 scattered around the files that we kind of followed every rabbit trail until we wound up at the current box—but I think it's the right one. Come see!"

I blew out a breath and walked down to her aisle. Iggy Risner and his little brother, Oz, were so intent on whatever stack of paper they were reading that neither one looked up. I cleared my throat and put my hands on my hips. Seemed like something I'd seen Ramos do to his teens.

Oz saw me first. He waved. "Hey, Mercury." Back to reading he went. You'd have thought I was the mailman.

What? Maybe I was expecting *some* notoriety.

Iggy's head popped up next. His eyes went wide. He scrambled onto his feet so fast his sneakers squeaked on the tile floor. "Mercury! This is so cool! We got a ride over in our own truck by some grumpy old guy who didn't like Oz's jokes. Have you seen the stuff that's in these boxes? There's so many top-secret things, but don't worry. Liz got us badges and everything!"

He was pulling on a lanyard. I grimaced. A badge dangled from the end, half black and half white, with the bland words "Essential Employee" printed atop the Procyon logo. Looked like my nightmare vision of my next meeting with Alvarez was coming true. Somewhere upstairs Edith was probably chuckling. "That's great, Iggy. Really great."

"Wait until I tell you about all the stuff we saw at Area 51! Remember? I was telling you on the phone before we fought those soda monsters—"

"Look, I'd be glad to hear about every word once this is over with."

Oz snorted. "Don't worry, he won't ever shut up about it."

"Zip it, Oz," Iggy hissed.

Oz mouthed the words *Zip it, Oz,* and went back to reading.

"Take it easy, guys." I crouched with them. Liz had already settled back into her spot, where she was rifling through papers in the box that seemed to be the object of everyone's attention. The label read "Project Domesticate." Huh. "But we've got bigger problems. So, bring me up to speed on Site 17."

"It's all right here." Liz's tone became positively professorial. "Site 17 was opened in 1977 with one purpose: To stabilize a rip and hold it open."

She said it so simply but that didn't stop the words

from squeezing me like an astral fiend's icy grip. "You've gotta be kidding me."

"I wish I was. But . . . Well, let me back up." She lifted a sheet with a faded Polaroid. A rusty paperclip had put a crease through the top but I could still make out the subject's face. The guy had wavy hair and a thick mustache. Man. If I hadn't known the project took place in the 1970s, I sure would have guessed from his hairdo and clothes. "Dr. Daniel Wayland. He was head of Procyon's research division back then, looking into the first readings anyone could electronically get on the rips."

"He was our tachyon pioneer, it sounds like."

"He was." For as nerdy as the talk was getting, Liz sounded like she'd just been told Procyon was shutting Cyril down for good. "So, this was back when Wilhelmina was the brand-new operative. She took out an astral fiend that appeared through a rip in the Arbor Valley in the summer of 1976. I guess there was an old barn or something like that in the woods. Anyway, not long after, the forecaster at the time, Rhoda Pathkiller—Edith's grandmother—had an odd vision."

"Don't know about you, Liz, but all the visions I've had with Forecasters have been odd."

"Yeah, I know, but this one was odd because of the where and when." Liz frowned. "Boys, the map?"

"Yep, got it here." Iggy plucked another sheet from Oz's

hands.

"Hey, I was memorizing that!"

"You'll get it back."

"Not if your grubby hands mess it up."

"They're not grubby! Liz made us wash and wear gloves, bonehead."

Oz wrinkled his nose. "I'm telling Mom."

"Guys." I pinched the bridge of my nose. "Maps for everybody, later. Liz?"

"The new vision revealed another rip was going to appear three years later in the same place." Liz's eyes grew wide again. "It sounds like, from these reports, that hardly anybody took Dr. Wayland seriously but he still got some support, enough that they let him quietly construct a containment facility on the grounds of the old barn."

"Site 17." I gazed at the map, which was a grainy color aerial photo. Sure enough, there was a barn there. I imagined a tiny Sherry Jean Crown—aka Wilhelmina—at the top of her game, a young twenty-something, slashing at an astral fiend with the pulsar stave.

"Got it!" Iggy brandished another photo as if it were a pirate sword.

"Gently." I cradled it with way more care, because the thing was already crumpled on one edge, hopefully from storage and not from the kid.

There was Wayland, looking more haggard than in his

mugshot. He was standing inside a big, dark room, smiling.

Behind him rose a metal frame that looked like a lopsided diamond with wire wrapped around each side in varying depths. I wondered why it looked familiar until it slapped me in the face: The shape was one of the parallelograms of the Procyon logo.

"The rip opened on schedule," Liz said, "But before any fiend could come out, Wayland started his device and—wham! The rip stayed put. Nothing came through."

"Please don't tell me they sent people through, either, from our end."

Liz shook her head. "The notes are redacted in a lot of places but I can make out enough to tell they couldn't get anything to pass through this rip, no matter how hard they tried. Wayland's notes continue for eighteen months and then—nothing."

"Nothing?"

"There's no more pages. One sheet details a new round of power fluctuations Wayland was monitoring. And that's it. Whatever happened at Site 17, Procyon got rid of all evidence."

"Okay." I rubbed my chin. "But this Wayland guy could still be alive, right? Even if the last notes were from, what, 1981 or so."

"Nope," Oz said. "He's dead."

The three of us looked at him. Oz seemed puzzled by the attention. He pointed at the papers scattered before him. Lots were diagrams of a building, down to the ventilation ducts, like he was trying to figure out where John McClane crawled from. "What? That's what this says. Pretty sad. He was probably somebody's dad or grandpa."

Dr. Wayland. Older by a few years, looking tired, or even sad.

The notation underneath read, "Presumed deceased, August 10, 1981."

My phone buzzed. I blinked, then read the message.

<Give me half an hour and I can be there.>

It was Dominic.

I glanced back at the photo of Dr. Wayland, then at the schematics scattered around us. *What exactly did you do out there in the woods, Doc, and where did that put Harry?*

Chapter Fourteen

Lily Beausoleil

The t-shirt that Procyon gave Lily was too loose-fitting. She tied it off so it didn't feel like a baggy dress. It was a simple thing, but it was the only action she could do to control the situation - otherwise everything about the day felt so out of her grasp. Even after their supernatural adventures saving San Francisco from an angry dark spirit, being in another dimension hit different.

And now they had lost Harry. He'd tried to port her out of the way of that soda fountain beast, and the glitches they experienced in this realm must have thrown him off. He took the blows meant for her, and in the midst of the confusion he disappeared.

Sarah Jane had healed the other injuries that she and Demarcus had suffered, even if they'd refrained from telling Procyon about her abilities, but the pain in her heart couldn't be fixed so easily.

The staff worked at their high-tech computer stations, an electronic hum faintly moving through the air. They hadn't seen Mercury for a while now, and they kept to themselves at a few spare desks in the back of the room. Demarcus stared gloomily at the floor. She couldn't remember him sitting so still in the time she'd known him. SJ flipped through a guide of San Camillo.

Lily absently pulled out her phone. No signal. Stupid cell plans. Why wouldn't they cover interdimensional roaming?

On second thought, her dad might ground her for life with that bill.

A door opened and Mercury strode into the room, followed by the computer gal Liz and the two kids that had shown up at the soda museum. Iggy? Oz? Where did those names come from?

The two kids chattered excitedly. Lily felt a pang, thinking about her brother who'd died in the same accident that claimed her mother. She didn't realize how much she missed the constant noise Luke spouted.

While Mercury and Liz stopped at her computer station, Demarcus jumped up and stomped toward the two. Lily swallowed. Before she could say anything, he put his hand on Mercury's shoulder and spun the operative to face him.

This wasn't like him.

"Look, I don't know what you guys are doing around here, but our friend disappeared and nothing's happening to find him," Demarcus snapped.

Mercury put his hand up like he was about to shove Demarcus back, but he stopped himself. "Back off, kid. I know what it's like to lose someone you care about. But when you guys showed up at the museum, it messed up a situation that I had under control. No one invited you."

Lily and SJ hurried over while the two continued to argue. "We saved your butt. It took all of us, even these guys," Demarcus gestured towards Iggy and Oz. "Don't tell me you had it 'under control.'"

Iggy beamed while Oz stared at Sarah Jane. Did his cheeks turn a little red?

Mercury stuck a finger up and opened his mouth before he paused. Then he pulled out the pulsar stave. "You guys did help. But this is the tool that takes care of these creatures, and I'm the one who wields it."

Before he could blink, Demarcus had snatched it from his hand and the stave blazed to life. Lily couldn't fully tell what kind of energy came from the pulsar stave, but she felt something tug at her power when it was lit.

"Yeah, despite what your techs say, I can light it up too. Maybe you're not so special," Demarcus said.

The whole room froze, and the tension settled over everyone. Mercury narrowed his eyes. "Put. That. Down.

That's your only warning."

Before Demarcus could reply, Sarah Jane put her hand on his arm. "Demarcus, you need to step back. What would John say? What's our strength? This isn't going to help Harry."

The crackling buzz of the pulsar stave was the only sound for a few seconds. Lily wanted to reach out with her light manipulation, to see if she could interact with it. Her fingers rose . . .

Demarcus extinguished the stave and the room took a collective breath. He handed the metal cylinder to Mercury. "I'm sorry. Something here has me on edge. I know you want to figure things out too."

Mercury tucked the weapon away. "It's okay, kid. Crazy circumstances do equally crazy things to any of us. We have been working on a lead, and I've got a friend who has skills similar to Harry that's coming soon. I promise, we'll do all we can."

Lily relaxed with the newly brokered peace.

Liz sat at her computer, Cyrus was it? "There's an anomaly at Site 17, and that's where we need to focus. At least, we think so."

A Procyon employee came over to Mercury when he signaled. "I don't want to put you at risk, but I know you can handle yourselves, and we want you there when we find Harry," Mercury said. "But promise me you'll follow my lead. Not because I'm older—but because this is my world. I've been fighting these things for a while. If I ever find myself on your Earth, I'll return the favor."

An increasingly excited Iggy bounced next to Mercury. "This is awesome! Our first official mission. And not just with Mercury, but with . . . you guys. Do you have a name?"

Before anyone else could answer, Mercury made a slash move across his throat. "Absolutely not. Look," he rubbed his temple, apparently not sure how to handle being a super youth pastor figure. "I appreciate what you guys did at the museum and the vault, but this is dangerous work. These guys have powers and they need to be there for Harry. You'll need to stay here. Got it?"

The look on Iggy's face broke Lily's heart. He seemed crushed. But Oz and Sarah Jane had stepped to the side and were whispering. Lily and Demarcus shared a quizzical glance.

"I'll head to the equipment room and get things arranged. Hopefully by the time you're ready, Dominic will be here. We can head out then." As he headed off, Lily could hear him mutter, "Maybe then I can get some Carlito's pizza."

Demarcus knelt down to be closer to Iggy's level. "Hey man, you were pretty wicked at the museum. You and Oz, it was brilliant using that explosive soda. But, we learned back in our world that sometimes you have to wait until you're ready to tackle a battle."

The boy's countenance brightened. "Yeah, maybe you're right. It's just, Mercury is my hero. I try to ask myself 'what would Mercury do' when we're having our adventures back home."

Liz whispered, "What have we done?" in a regretful tone.

Sarah Jane waved for all of them to join her and Oz in a corner. "What's up?" Lily asked.

"This is going to sound weird, but as I've been praying about Harry's situation, I really feel like Iggy and Oz have a role to play. And Oz has some information to share."

Iggy flashed red. "You're not going to tell them about my feelings for Jenn, are you?"

That got Oz giggling. He almost blurted something out, but SJ held up a stern finger and he swallowed whatever he'd planned to say. Then he collected himself. "When we looked at the papers about this site, I saw some plans that showed some vents to what looked like a control room thingie or something. I think you might need a couple of people small enough to get in there."

They all stared at the two kids. Who knew what was going on, but Sarah Jane had a real gift of discernment. She and Demarcus had learned to trust her.

"That's all good, but Mercury was pretty adamant he wanted them here. How do we get around that?" Demarcus asked.

Sarah Jane gasped and pointed at Lily. She suddenly knew what prompted that outburst. "Demarcus, do you remember when I snuck up on you at the ren faire earlier? It wasn't just me being stealthy. Lily practiced a new trick with her light. She made me nearly invisible."

His mouth dropped. "I was wondering how you managed that! Do you think you could do that to these guys?"

Lily grinned as she considered the two energetic boys. "You guys want to disappear for a bit?"

Harry Wales

The walk seemed like it took forever. Harry was reminded of that scene from the *Holy Grail* where the knight kept running and running and never got any closer. But, there was nothing in this crazy place except the fuzzy shape of a human that finally drew near.

What would happen next, though? Was the person friend or foe? Harry realized with a start that maybe they're the reason he was brought here.

There was a faint sound growing louder. He tried to concentrate, readying himself for fight or flight. If nothing else, he could port somewhere. He hoped.

The shape focused. A man in a trench coat. Or, a lab

coat? His features blurred, but Harry could make out dark, wavy hair and a mustache. Either that, or the guy had a fat sausage on his face.

Why'd I think about food again?

And the noise he heard was a song. Where had he heard that melody before?

"Uh, hey? Where am I? And why are you fuzzy-looking?" Harry did a face palm with the last sentence. That's not the best way to put a good foot forward. More like into the mouth.

The man slowly looked up, then around. Then he groaned, holding his abdomen before getting back to his small panel in front of him. He seemed distracted, muttering, "That's strange. But I need to figure out these calculations to fix my machine. I'm so close. Those last incursions made progress. I've almost got the rip stabilized."

Harry realized the guy was mumbling to himself. He missed seeing Harry, and started back humming his song. Then he sang the chorus.

"Staying alive, staying alive . . ."

Chapter Fifteen

Mercury Hale

Light flared in the Tracking office. I shielded my eyes against the expanding bubble. Every piece of paper in the place fluttered but didn't fly off. Kudos to Liz for binge-buying clear acrylic paperweights with the Procyon logo nestled inside.

A guy's silhouette formed out of the swirling colors. The howling winds died out, leaving behind Dominic Zein. His gold tie flapped against its tack.

"Mercury." Dominic smiled. He smoothed out black hair with the side of his hand. Dominic had the sleek good looks of a young Hollywood actor, like that guy who'd played the live action Aladdin. "Good to see you."

"Same, man." We shook hands. I expected the glow from the Echo Watches on his wrists to burn, but all I got was a soft buzz, like from a cell phone. The relics' pieces quit spinning and fit back together, forming twin bands of antique metal.

"Sorry I couldn't come sooner. I was wrapping up another capture." He tapped the rectangular bulge in his shirt pocket.

Right. The deck of cards bearing pictures of the next dimension's Most Wanted. "Anybody we know?"

"Let's just say a certain influencer's about to have zero influence."

"Good to know." My conversational skills were about as good as a middle school boy eating lunch at a table full of girls. Hey, you try finding a way to explain what's been going on. "So, about other dimensions . . ."

I gestured at the teen standing at the back of Tracking. Wait a sec. Two? Where was the quiet girl? Sarah Somebody. And there was no sign of Lily either. I sighed. "Meet Demarcus."

"Nice to meet you." Dominic nodded. "I'm supposed to help you find your friend."

"We really appreciate it." I glanced at Demarcus. "Don't we?"

"Yeah. You bet." Demarcus had his arms folded. He lifted his chin but wasn't about to make eye contact with me. Probably he was still embarrassed by our headbutting contest a few minutes ago. It didn't help that his arguments had stirred up every doubt I'd buried.

Who was I to be leading this operation?

"Where are you from?" Dominic asked.

"Um . . ." Demarcus glanced at me. "San Francisco."

Dominic gave me that look. You know which one. The one of an older brother trying to figure out what I'd screwed up.

"Not our San Francisco," I added.

"I see." Dominic, who was dressed like he'd stepped out of a corporate office—and probably had—loosened his stance. Not so subtle. He expected a fight.

Problem was, so did Demarcus. Heck, they were super-heroes on their world. Demarcus vibrated until his solid lines went blurry.

"Easy, kid." I held up my hand. "Dominic, he's not from *that* Earth. Another one. Much nicer."

"All right. If you say so. I was wondering how they'd arrived from San Francisco when it's been destroyed."

"What?" Demarcus was suddenly two feet from us.

"Mercury . . ." Dominic's face was a stiff mask.

"I said, easy." I blew out a breath. "Dominic runs under the code name 'Gemini.' There's an Alternate Earth in which the West Coast has been trashed for eighty years, but the people there who're still upset about it keep sending doppelgangers to cause havoc here. Dominic nabs them."

"So, he teleports, sort of like Harry." Demarcus pointed. "With his bracelets."

"Armbands." Dominic frowned. "The Echo Watches."

"Fancy."

"Thanks. But how did you, ah, just . . . move fast?"

"It's complicated, sort of," Demarcus said. "The easy way to say it is none of us need weapons or devices. Our powers are God's gift."

"God's . . ." Dominic shook his head and looked at me. "I'd ask you to explain but I gather there's more at stake."

"Like always." I pointed to the main screen and the big map Liz had left in place. "The other kid—Harry—tele-ported right between dimensions."

"Between them, how?"

"Beats me. Some space that exists 'between' here and the Interstice, or at least that's how Liz explained it, com-plete with air quotes. Plus side: We roughly know where he is. Minus side: We need you to grab him while the rest of us figure out how to shut down a rip that's been locked open since the seventies."

Dominic's eyes widened but at least he stopped asking questions I didn't feel qualified to answer. "Then I'd better get him back. You said you can track him, correct?"

I handed him one of the oval devices Liz had fashioned a few years ago when Loredana and Ramos had fallen through a dimensional barrier. It was black and silver. Five notches on the black side held tiny lights. "Stick this on the back of your phone. It's tuned to the trackers on the kids."

"Tracking devices? Really?" Demarcus sighed.

"Throttle back, Kid Flash," I muttered. "They're in the bottoms of your shoes. Apparently you stepped on them when you walked into Tracking the first time, right after you helped me out against the playground creature. Liz was just being cautious. We've had enough history with people who like to try to kill us breaking in."

"Yeah, okay. I get it. But you could have told us." He had his hands on his hips. "Should have told us. I think we've earned the right."

I wanted to snap at the kid but, again, he made a good point. "I know you have. Be patient with me, okay?"

"At least I didn't try to take the glow stick again." Demarcus smirked.

I chuckled. "Sure. We'll call it an improvement. Dominic, are you good?"

"One moment." He held the modified phone aloft. The bottom three notches glowed green and the fourth flickered. "You know I usually transit to places I've seen, at least in pictures, or from a description."

"Sorry, Dominic, but we're fresh out of pics from the unknown dimension."

He gazed at the phone. His other hand rubbed the crease in his slacks between his thumb and forefinger. Nervous habit? "What about a picture of Harry?"

"Here you go." Demarcus swiped through his own phone and held up the screen so Dominic could see the smiling kid. "Except he's wearing a wizard's robe. I think he ditched the beard though."

"A robe?" Dominic blinked at me. I just shrugged.

"Long story," Demarcus said.

"All right." Dominic took a picture with his phone, which I guessed was smarter than asking Demarcus to send it to him, since the Anointed's cell phones probably had dropped service. "This should help—though I'll be honest with you all, the outcome isn't looking great."

"God won't abandon us," Demarcus said. "Or Harry. I know you'll find him."

Dominic's smile seemed sincere but, frankly, a little sad.

"You okay?" I asked.

"I am. I was just wishing I still had the faith he's showing. It could be this work is wearing down the hope I'd thought I'd found again." Dominic's smile faded. "But if you'll pray for us, Demarcus, I think that will help a lot."

"You've got it." Demarcus closed his eyes. So did Dominic.

I wasn't expecting church in Tracking, but I'd hung around Ramos long enough to know it was important to people like them. People who believed and proved their beliefs with their actions.

Besides, I'd thrown enough silent entreaties at the sky—along with plenty of not-so-silent versions—I wasn't about to begrudge them.

We needed all the help we could get.

"All right." Dominic stepped back from us and put the phone with its attached tracker into his pocket. Then he frowned, loosened his tie, and handed it to me in a neat bundle. "Hold onto this, will you? If I lose one of these that Jess bought for me she's threatened to staple it to my collar."

"No problem." I took the tie. "Good luck."

"Godspeed."

He held out his arms. The Echo Watches broke apart into their spinning components. The wind and light built in reverse of his arrival, and in seconds, he disappeared.

"Okay." I ran a hand through my hair and set the tie on a nearby desk. Hmm. I put a paperweight on top. Better. "Road trip."

We rolled out of Procyon in two silver SUVs. Yes, both had tinted windows. Yes, I knew it was cliché. But there was no way I was taking myself in full costume, plus three teenagers, and six security guys off campus in full view of our round-the-clock protestors.

Nobody said much during the ride, especially not

Sarah Jane, who we'd found down in the garage talking with Garvey. She was still blushing, like I was gonna send her to her room without supper. Seriously? If I had a problem with her tardiness I'd be this dimension's biggest hypocrite.

Our convoy got on the 311 heading out of San Camillo. The highway threaded through the suburbs, past the farms, and into the forests. There were still plenty of scorched areas up in the hills that one of the many dimensional incursions had caused.

I was getting sick and tired of him leaving his mark. At least this time we weren't dealing with him, not directly, but I could still feel him sneering at me, like Dr. Wayland's mess could have the Whisperer's fingers in it.

Or maybe it was his whispers that had prodded Wayland to his doom.

"Left turn coming up." Garvey was driving. The first SUV drove off onto a bumpy, overgrown road that was more like a rutted path. Garvey followed, hands tight on the steering wheel.

Somebody yelped. One of the kids? I glanced back. Sarah Jane blushed again, except this time, she hurriedly rubbed her head. "I bumped the ceiling."

Klutzy teen superheroes. That's what I needed. "You guys had better be more careful once we get—"

"Target in sight."

And it was. We came out of the last of several twists and turns onto a broad patch of asphalt. Weeds poked through every few feet. Trees crowded the crumbling edges.

I got out of the SUV. Summer heat soaked me. Man. I wished the suit came with air conditioning.

A single-story building of grimy, taupe concrete hunkered on the other side of the asphalt. Bronzed windows reflected our SUVs and the wings of birds that flitted by. Their chirps were the only sounds.

Site 17.

"Secure the perimeter," Garvey ordered.

Six security men and women fanned out around the building, their boots crunching on broken glass in front and through the undergrowth out back. Garvey approached the shattered front door, his MP5 submachine gun at the ready.

I pressed the earbud beneath my mask. "You there, Liz?"

A pair of drones buzzed overhead. "We're ready," she said. "This is the source, without a doubt. I'm picking up the same tachyonic disturbances as we've seen at each incident today."

"Standing by, sir," Garvey said. "On your signal."

I glanced back at the Anointed. "Then let's go see what Project Domesticate looks like these days." I was pretty sure I sounded like a boss.

That didn't stop my guts from twisting as I stepped into the dark lobby.

Chapter Sixteen

Dominic Zein

This isn't who I'm supposed to be.

My parents raised Dominic Zein for an architect's career. Success was paramount. Little else mattered—certainly not their marriage. Rising above their humble roots took precedence.

And yet, for the past five years, it seems all I've done is run from catastrophe to catastrophe. Gone are the hours I could devote to the sweeping lines of a new building. I complete one project a year, if I'm fortunate.

But I try to not harbor bitterness toward this destiny. That's the only way I can reconcile my new life. At least Jess and I are together. The dark moments when I thought we'd part ways still haunt me.

Your soul is your own, Dominic. Our Lord in Heaven made it specifically, without a concern as to what other souls are like. When he knit you together, he put in you that mysterious spark that he placed into no other.

I smile. Funny Father Hamra's words should return to me now, in this place.

Though as I look around at the formless, sunlit expanse, maybe it shouldn't be so surprising. I've never encountered a space quite like it, and given how many dimensions I've transited between as Mercury Hale's taxi service, one would assume I'd have amassed a greater catalog.

There's more of the dull bitterness. I shake my head as if it will drop free into the ghostly grass I'm walking through. The Echo Watches can take me anywhere in the world, and anywhere on other worlds, for that matter. Procyon Foundation relies on me to get operatives from one place to another, quickly, and with good reason: We need every tactical advantage we can gather in this interdimensional Cold War that often turns hot.

Still.

There are days when I'd rather etch the perfect lines for a soaring structure in the quiet of my office or on the benches under the aspen leaves rustling in the park.

Purpose. I've found mine. I'm still learning to be content.

The tracking device affixed to my phone rumbles. The lights are four bright now, with the fifth flickering. I'm near Harry, though how "near" translates in this eerie dimension that's simultaneously blinding and shadowed is beyond my understanding.

I walk on, adjusting my course as the lights flicker and flash. Eventually they're solid green, all five of them, and I can see why.

There's a silhouette ahead. The outline of a man in a long coat fades in and out of my perception. I scowl and squint, as if I'm trying to see an airplane in a sunny sky. "Hello? Harry?"

The man glances over his shoulder. His coat is, I now realize, a laboratory coat. He has a thick mustache and wavy hair, which both seem unkempt for someone wearing a tie. The man seems to look past my right shoulder. "I've clearly been working too long and too late," he mutters. There's a peculiar buzzing around his words, like static through a badly tuned radio. "It doesn't matter. The stabilization is holding, as it has for months now, but there's so much more to accomplish. I must sound like a lunatic, talking to myself, but this tape recording is vital to the documentation of the process. Once Procyon understands—"

Dr. Daniel Wayland. Mercury's briefing notes, if his scribbles can be called that, mention he was the one who held a rip open. Eighteen months. The idea makes me suddenly sick. None of these portals are supposed to be permanently open. They exist and have a purpose, but if we jam our foot in the door, won't that risk letting all manner of evil in?

I've seen what comes through, and not just monsters.

One time, it was me.

Wayland's words disappear in a roar of static. He shields himself from something I can't see, then fades to an indistinct shadow.

"Hello? Is somebody else there?"

The voice is younger. It sounds as if it's coming from the end of an auditorium, but a quarter of the way through my turn, I spot a teenager emerging from the mist. He's pale and his eyes are wide. He walks toward me out of our misty surroundings with gentle steps that remind me of treading with Sammy across the frozen Van River in winter.

"You're . . . solid." He frowns. "Are you here with us?"

"It seems so." I touch his shoulder, partly to reassure him and partly to reassure me. The wizard's robe was startling, I have to admit, but at least Demarcus had warned me. "My name's Dominic. Mercury Hale sent me."

"Dominic." He sighs, his breath shaky. "I'm Harry. It's really nice to see another face that isn't a shadow."

"I can imagine."

"How long have I been here?"

"A few hours." I took a quick turn, taking in our disorienting surroundings.

"It feels like days. Did you bring anything to eat?"

What was it with teenagers and food? Was I that ravenous? "Sorry. But I did bring a way out of here."

"That's great. My powers . . . I don't know how much they told you back at Procyon, but I can teleport from place to place. That's what I was doing when we wound up in your dimension—in San Camillo. And I got stuck here when I tried to use them to teleport to safety."

"No luck leaving, I take it."

Harry shakes his head. "And I wasn't sure that I should, not until I could talk to him."

He points toward the shady apparition, which is solidifying again. This time Wayland's expression is one of complete bewilderment, not the studious concentration I'd first witnessed, and he looks more substantial, too.

"Who are you?" Wayland asks. "How did you get into this facility?"

Harry and I look at each other. He takes a sidestep nearer to me. "Dr. Daniel Wayland, my name is Dominic Zein. I work for Procyon Foundation.

"Procyon? Did they send you because . . ." His eyes widen and I realize he's finally taking in our full surroundings. "This isn't the site. Where is the rip?"

"Doctor, what's the last thing you remember?"

"I was changing the modulation of the rip stabilization ring. The RSR had held the rip open for so many months but I was unable to get any telemetry back from probes I launched through its aperture." Wayland scowls. "There has to be a way to modulate the very structure of the rip itself."

"That's . . . Not possible." I blurt the words before I consider the consequences. The rips are, for whatever way in which they bend and warp space-time, natural occurrences.

"It *is* possible." The last word punches through the air in a wave that brushes my hair and ripples my shirt. Harry alters his stance, a bit like his friends at Procyon did, but I can't figure out how he's planning to fight. "You don't know what you're talking about. Typical Procyon bean-counters. Budgets and public perception are what you care about, not the elemental forces holding the universe together."

"I think, Dr. Wayland, you're forgetting who fashioned those forces and for what purpose." I lower my arms so the Echo Watches are visible. They begin to glow. "I need you to come with me. None of us are meant to stay here."

"Here . . ." His eyes widen further. The color, such as it is, drains from his face. "Did it work? It must have worked. I entered the calculations and . . . But, wait. This place."

"Dr. Wayland." I step toward him. If I'm near enough, the portal effect of the Echo Watch can remove him from this place with me and Harry when we depart. This is the part of the extraction that sets my nerves on edge—the seconds before I strike. Though I've got to admit, there's a thrill, too, that I won't admit to anyone else. "The last steps of your experiment . . . They took place in 1981, didn't they?"

"Of course it's 1981." Wayland's frown deepens. I get the feeling he views me as dimmer than his worst student.

"Nineteen eighty-one?" Harry gasps. "How long has he been here?"

Wayland grasps the front of Harry's robe—but he's still standing in front of me. The two Waylands are fuzzier, though, rendered insubstantial by their separation. Simultaneously another wave shoves me back. I don't stop until I dig in my heels, which amuses me a bit because I can't tell how real the physical sensation beneath my shoes is.

"When is this?" The Waylands' voices bounce off each other in anger-fueled distortion. He pulls Harry nearer. "What year?"

"Let him go." There's no sense negotiating. My tone is the same with which I scold Sammy when he's been a bad dog. I raise my arms. The Echo Watches spin and crackle, eager to discharge the bursts of energy that will knock Wayland senseless. "You've been considered dead for forty years."

It's the wrong move.

Wayland flings Harry at me. I catch him and we're sent

tumbling. So much for my attempt to subdue him with the Echo Watches, I'm sorry—I've never practiced the scenario in which I have to intercept a flying teenager.

"Get me out of here!" Wayland coalesces with himself. His eyes glow purple as the rest of the space around him darkens. He reaches out on either side and curls his fingers.

The dimension itself wrinkles in his grasp.

Chapter Seventeen

Iggy Risner

Life is somewhat like a video game, full of thrilling twists, turns, and surprise power-ups. My plan was simple: level up and enjoy the ride, just like in the neighborhood where I'm sort of a hero, always rescuing others and basking in a bit of local fame. However, this vacation has revealed a new purpose for my investigative skills—Mercury's plea for help made it clear I may be needed elsewhere.

On our way to Site 17, the road turned into a wild roller coaster ride. The jolting and bouncing had Oz let out a small yelp, earning us a strange look from Mercury, but luckily we were still invisible and Sarah Jane covered for us.

I couldn't believe my luck—a secret Procyon site! My mind raced with excitement, envisioning this adventure as a perfect addition to my case files back home. My only concern was keeping us a secret from Mercury; he couldn't find out we were here. I nudged Oz lightly to remind him to stay quiet.

"Keep it down," I whispered.

"I'm trying," Oz hissed. "But I bumped my head."

As we arrived and stepped out of the silver SUVs, I couldn't help but think that our top-secret organization needed a more official image—black cars would be much cooler and scream "top secret" way better than silver ones. I made a mental note to speak to Mercury about this soon. Silver just screamed amateurish.

The building at Site 17 was a neglected mess with weeds and vines taking over. I cringed, thinking about how this would drag down the property value. I know all about property value and how unkept yards are an eyesore to potential buyers. My dad, the Home Owners Association president of Whispering Pines, would be horrified.

"Secure the perimeter," Garvey barked, and the security guys spread out. We cautiously entered the dark and eerie lobby.

My excitement got the better of me, and I ended up bumping into Mercury. He shot a look at Demarcus, but the light manipulation skills of Lily kept Oz and myself hidden. I scurried to the back behind the group.

Amidst the tension, Oz's annoyance couldn't be suppressed. "Hey, Iggy? Want a soda?"

"Seriously, Oz?" I hissed. "Why would I want a soda

right now? We're here to help out. So stay sharp."

"Suit yourself," Oz replied, and I heard the pop of the soda can and a light fizz.

"Ugh, Oz?" I asked. "Where did you get the soda?"

"From the museum," Oz said. "Duh!"

"Oz, I don't think you should drink that soda."

"Ugh, that's disgusting."

A quiet hush fell across the room, followed by an unexpected sound slipping out, like skin flapping quickly and fast.

"Seriously, Mercury—" Garvey started but then quickly cut off. When I spun around Garvey, along with all six security officers, lay on the floor.

"What happened?" Demarcus asked.

"I think I know exactly what happened." I turned and saw Mercury staring down at me.

"Uh, hi, Mercury," I said. "What's up, man?"

"Iggy! How did you and Oz get here?" Mercury pinched the bridge of his nose in frustration.

"It was Lily," Oz said. "She used this crazy light trick to make us invisible."

"Forget that," Demarcus chimed in. "Oz, you just managed to incapacitate our entire security detail."

"Oz! Strawberry Wind! What were you thinking?"

"I think this soda is disgusting," Oz said. "That's not what I thought I was drinking."

"What?" I asked. "What did you think you were drinking?"

"I thought it was invisible grape," Oz said. "I thought it would be cool to be invisible."

"You already were invisible!"

Oz gave me a funny look. "Oh, yeah. I forgot."

Amidst the chaos, Sarah Jane laughed and patted Oz on the head.

As Demarcus eyed the half-can of soda in his hand, curiosity brimming in his eyes, I winced inwardly, knowing what might come next. "So how does it work?" he asked, oblivious to the impending disaster. "Do you just drink it?"

"Uh, Demarcus," I tried to warn him, but it was too late.

With a brave gulp, Demarcus downed the soda, and the room fell silent for a split second before chaos erupted. The mixture of flavors hit his taste buds like an atomic blast, and he let out a noise that could rival a thousand trumpets in a symphony.

The sound shook the ground, rattling everything around us.

"Earthquake!" Oz screamed and hid behind Sarah Jane.

I could practically taste the fizzy soda particles in the air as I struggled to avoid getting a whiff. Meanwhile, Lily, the quick thinker, darted around Demarcus as if she was avoiding a cannonball of toxic wind.

The security dudes, still unconscious from Oz's earlier soda incident, didn't stand a chance against Demarcus's sonic emission. If they were out cold before, they were now snoozing through an explosive serenade.

Amidst the rumbling aftermath, Mercury leaned his head against a support pole in the shadows, his face a perfect mix of disbelief and stress. He looked like he was contemplating life's mysteries.

"Hey Iggy," Oz chimed in. "Since he's a speedster, do you think that smell traveled faster than light?"

When I glanced back Mercury was lightly banging his head against the pole asking: "Why?"

Chapter Eighteen

Mercury Hale

You've got to be kidding me.

There we were, stepping into danger, and I was back in charge of babysitting while my *entire security team* was knocked out by fart soda.

I can't even believe I just said "fart soda."

"Um." Demarcus held his hand to his mouth like he was trying not to barf. "Do we wanna move these guys outside?"

I sighed. "That'd be great."

He grabbed Garvey and his men one at a time, zipping them out to the parking lot. Iggy and Oz watched and, mercifully, didn't say anything or hand out weaponized soft drinks.

Whatever. I kept a firm grip on the pulsar stave and used it like a giant flashlight, which was handy because apparently Procyon wasn't paying the electric bill anymore.

Its golden light cast deep shadows in the darkness.

We navigated the hallways in a close group—me at the front, Lily and Sarah Jane with the boys in the middle, Demarcus bringing up the rear. We took a couple of blind turns down tight corridors. Our shoes crunched on broken glass and crumpled paper. It got even darker the deeper inside we went.

I was wishing there was a way to dial up the light from the stave when a softer glow reflected on the walls ahead. I glanced back.

"I thought you could use the help," Lily whispered. Her hands were a brilliant white.

"Wow," Iggy said. "That's super cool."

"Yeah. Even cooler than the pulsar stave," Oz murmured.

Iggy glared at him like he'd just dropped a "your mama" joke. "It is *not*."

"Zip it, you two." I tried to keep the frustration out of my voice but, honestly, I didn't try that hard. The kids meant well, and so did the Anointed teens, but seriously, how was I supposed to stop this portal from ripping things apart if I was chasing six youngsters around?

They were my responsibility, though. Like I'd told Ramos. Maybe if I repeated it enough, I'd start believing I could get it right.

All right, Mercury. Think of them as your team. Your

job is to get them in and out, alive. And stop things from getting worse in the process.

"Oh," Sarah Jane breathed.

I looked up. We were stopped in front of a pair of broken double doors. The lab lay beyond the entrance.

The biggest rip I'd ever seen was writhing in the center.

The containment device was doing a lousy job of containing, because the two angular sections had broken apart. They weren't sealed together like in the old photo. Their busted sections dangled wires all over the place—slender coppery ones, thick black ones, and rippling silver ones. Dozens and dozens of them.

All of them waving in the air like they were caught in a breeze.

My guess was the swirling oval in the middle was the problem. The captured rip looked a lot like the ones I'd faced, and as we stood there gawking at it, I half expected a couple of astral fiends to come screaming out. No dice. Instead, I saw my distorted reflection on a glassy surface. There were stars behind it—stars, and planets, and cities. The views changed every few seconds, each picture melting into the next.

"What did they do?" Lily asked.

"Something they shouldn't have," I said. "Something nobody should have. It's a stabilized rip, which I thought meant we'd be peeking into the stormy hellscape of the Interstice itself. Instead, we're getting . . . I'm not sure what."

"It looks like . . . Everywhere," Sarah Jane said. "So beautiful."

"Any chance one of those is our San Francisco?" Demarcus joined me at the front of our entourage. He lifted his chin as he scanned the entire room, like he was checking out every corner from where we stood. Good idea.

"No idea, but let's check in with the lady who knows all and sees all." I tapped my earbud. "Hey, Liz. How're things looking from up there?"

"Drones Seven and Eight are in position over Site 17." Liz sounded like she had marbles in her mouth—crunchy marbles.

"Are you . . . snacking?"

"Well, okay, Garvey made a run down to the Promenade early today and got some of the caramel popcorn we—"

"Nope. Stop. Literally the last straw." I held up my hands, fully aware Liz couldn't see me through the ceiling. "You need to save some for me."

"But there's—"

"Liz."

She sighed. "I will."

"At least two handfuls."

"I promise!" The crunching stopped. Plastic rustled through the earbud and Liz cleared her throat. "Okay. The tachyon levels are in flux all around you and when I say in flux I mean they're rippling up and down the scale so much and I don't think I've ever seen anything like it before!"

I glanced back at the rest of the gang. The kids were staring wide-eyed at the undulating portal but the teens turned worried expressions toward me. Big surprise. I was the adult in the room. The only one, thanks to the fart soda.

So I couldn't let them down. Wasn't about to.

Of course, that's when the floor bucked under our feet like the worst case of turbulence ever.

I landed on my butt, one leg folded underneath—the intact leg. Pain shot through clear to the knee. Demarcus yelped and tumbled halfway back to the door. Lily went down just as fast, but Demarcus caught her with one arm before she could slam into the wall. Sarah Jane crashed into Iggy and Oz, turning the three of them into a tangle of arms and legs.

The bone-rattling moan that followed was just as bad and way creepier than an astral fiend's shriek. What the heck? Since when did a rip make any noise other than a rushing wind? They definitely didn't cause earthquakes.

"Um, Mercury?" Liz's voice jumped in pitch. "The rip is expanding and worse, it's pinching off more rips."

"Yeah. Yeah, I can see that." I stared into the maelstrom whirling in front of us as I helped Sarah Jane to her feet. Iggy and Oz had already leapt upright. Liz wasn't wrong. The rip had expanded to fill the bulk of the room, with its frame forming a crooked, yawning mouth. The mirrored surface had gone murky and opaque, except where purple bolts lanced across its surface.

It was like someone had run an electrical cable across a pond and got the best fireworks display ever from it.

"Look out!" Sarah Jane cried.

Objects whipped at us from the left side of the room. For one second, I thought an astral fiend had sprung through the rip and was slashing with its tentacles, but then I saw the glittering copper. The wires. They'd become twisted and serrated, and more importantly, they'd aimed themselves at my face.

I brought the pulsar stave up and shredded the first two with a few quick swipes. It wasn't enough to obliterate them but at least I could hold them at bay.

"There's a massive tachyon surge under the floor!" Liz shouted, and for once I didn't mind she was shouting, because the racket from the portal and the wire tentacles were hammering my head. "The building schematics show a huge space down there that's got to be the power source for the containment frame."

"Yeah, I got news for you!" I flipped backwards over a wire tentacle intent on bisecting me right above the belly button. I sliced through its width using the pulsar stave while I was still upside down, then ended the landing on one knee. *Ow.* I don't recommend superhero landings. "The frame isn't doing much framing!"

"Oh. Yeah, that makes sense. Oh!" A resounding slap echoed through the earbud, followed by the rattle of keyboard keys.

"Liz?" I spun around and found another tentacle stampeding straight for my face. Searing light blazed across my field of view, reducing the offending pseudo-appendage to a molten mess.

Lily was shooting, I don't know, blasts of light or some kind of energy Mr. Spock would find "fascinating" if he were describing them to the captain of the *USS Enterprise*. Fine by me.

The rip seemed to take a breather, as in, the tentacles slowed. It was like a giant, faceless Medusa trying to figure out who it wanted to kill first.

Me? I started shouting orders. I'm the kind of guy who isn't gonna stand around scratching his head when the monster in front of me decides to pull a silent monologue. "Demarcus! Get the kids out of here!"

"You got it!" Demarcus scooped up Iggy and Oz, who had a half second to look annoyed before the trio disappeared in a blur of speed. I swore I could still see their afterimage once they were gone.

"Okay. Lily? You take the right side. I'll take the left."

"What should I do?" She balled her hands into fists. Gotta say, the soft glow emanating around her was jaw-dropping. Ramos had once mentioned a Bible story about Moses in which he freaked out his people after talking with God because his face was lit up like a streetlamp. I got the same vibes.

"Just keep—blasting. With . . ." I gestured at her hands. "Those."

"Okay." The glow filled her eyes, too. Yikes.

"And Sarah Jane . . ." I frowned. Then I shut off my earpiece and stepped closer to her. "Time to level with me. What's your ability?"

"It's . . . I don't like revealing it to people I don't trust." She bit her lip. "But you've been looking out for us . . . I think God has given me peace about that."

I waited, worried if I mouthed off she might revoke that trust.

"I can heal injuries, even severe ones."

"Okay." I nodded. "That explains why you haven't been an active brawler. Well, let's run with that strategy and keep you in reserve. Sound good?"

"I'll stay out of the way and stand by if you need me." She was already on her way around the side of a shattered wall that I hoped would give her enough cover.

"Well, when it's me fighting, we're definitely talking about 'when' and not 'if,'" I muttered. The tentacles were whipping around faster but hadn't struck at us yet. Wasn't sure if that was a good or bad thing, but I was willing to bet the occasional earthquakes and the way the rip seemed to be bleeding off itself like soap bubbles propagating in the sink when I did dishes meant the latter. "Liz, what's the deal? Want to tell me what 'oh' is?"

"The power source below was designed by Dr. Wayland, too," she said. "It draws on tachyons leaking from the Interstice to power itself, but there's a flaw in the design that allows the rip to draw power from it, too, and away from the containment device. Or at least, that's what Cyril's calculations tell me."

"I'm not arguing with the supercomputer," I said, "So you're telling me if we shut it down, we not only cancel the containment but we kill the rip?"

"Probably."

I rolled my eyes. Always with the "probably."

"But the access tunnels are blocked by rubble. There's only one narrow path through the debris from the ladder just outside the building."

Great. More complications. And the rip emitted another ghastly moan. This one drove itself into the center of my head, like the world's worst brain freeze. Lily and Sarah Jane cried out. Pretty sure I did, too. It didn't help that I saw awful images of death from throughout the battles I'd had over the past three years—astral fiends draining people into mummies, others mutating into hideous creatures.

Demarcus appeared at my side. He stumbled a bit, his shoes skidding on the paper-strewn floor. The gust of wind and the *boom* that hit me a moment later almost slapped me into a wall. "What happened? I heard you guys yelling."

"This thing's past its warmup and ready for the main event." I looked him in the eyes. Scared, yeah, but so was I. And yet, we were both here. Ready to fight.

He and the others had shown me plenty of times they could handle responsibilities way more intense than I'd had to at their age. It was time I started treating them like that was true. I gave the pulsar stave a quick twist and separated it into two sizzling halves. "How about we get to work?"

I handed him one of the halves.

Demarcus flipped it end over end and caught it. Sparks skittered through the air. He grinned. "Let's do this."

Chapter Nineteen

Demarcus Bartlett

The pulsar stave blazed to life in Demarcus's hand. *Holy lightsaber!* He needed to seriously thank Mercury when this was over. He got how important the weapon was to the monster fighter, and it was an honor to wield it.

"Look out!"

The warning shouted by Sarah Jane saved him from being blinded. One of the flailing wire-tentacle things lashed in front of his face. The sting tore across his cheek, but if it weren't for his speed, his eyes would be toast. No more time for being a fanboy.

Demarcus swung the beacon of lightning at the wires a few times. He missed the first few times, but he started to understand the weight—or lack of—that the stave had. The metal handle had the heft, so it took him a minute to compensate for the energy part being weightless. Flashes zipped around as he started hacking off wires that got near him.

Was this what Lily felt like, using her light blasts?

Even though he started making regular contact with these swinging monstrosities, he didn't seem to be making any headway. He darted in and out from as close as he could get to the center of the . . . rip, as Mercury called it. There just didn't seem to be any progress. He stole a quick glance at Mercury, who did an impressive side flip to avoid being fileted by more tentacles.

Maybe if he flanked the thing, he could draw enough attention that Mercury could strike at the center.

He struggled to move at top speed, as a lot of equipment and debris littered the floor. Dodging around, he started to move away from Mercury. He passed an old-fashioned computer on a dusty metal desk. Something flickered on the screen . . .

A face lit up the screen, framed out of green pixels. Angry slanted eyebrows and an awkwardly laughing mouth froze him for a moment. Then a moaning sound emanated from his right. An ancient tape reel spun, causing more lights to flash and the freaky sound to fill the air.

The distraction proved costly. Pain seared across his back as wires raked down from an angle. Drops of blood and part of a dreadlock fell to the floor. Demarcus whipped around in anger, slashing more of the serrated wires. Out of his peripheral vision he saw Lily kneel down and, with her hands thrusted out, shot a light beam behind him. The tape reel exploded in a spray of sparks.

Lily Beausoleil

Lily made quick work of the creepy reel thing that caused Demarcus to get hurt. She marveled at how he always kept battling, even when she could see the gashes on his back.

As the glowing orb grew, purple lightning arced around the perimeter, and it seemed to bring to life any inanimate objects it contacted. Just like the soda museum. A folder started spitting out yellowed papers towards Mercury. He wasn't going to die by paper cut, but the sheets swirled in the maelstrom and forced him back before he got impaled by a razor point of a cable. Lily shot another blast off to stop that threat.

A voice sounded in her ear. "Hey, this isn't working. There's something else going on." Mercury tried to sound collected, but she thought she heard uncertainty in his voice. His half of the pulsar stave whirled through the air. Again, she felt the weapon call to her power. Her hand curled reflexively.

The crackling beam bent.

Mercury stopped and looked at the stave. Shook it for a moment. The energy straightened, but Lily had to believe that she could also sync with the pulsar stave for some rea-son.

"Mercury, the rip isn't slowing down," Liz said through the earbud, her voice starting to crackle with interference.

"Tell me something I don't know. Like how to do some-thing to actually affect this thing!" he replied.

The images on the surface of the rip undulated and flashed between different images. A galaxy of stars. Burned stumps and barren wasteland. A shadowy group of beings, glowing green. Then three men writhing amidst a swirl of energy. One of them wore a wizard's robe.

Harry?

A band of energy sprouted from the sphere and struck in front of her, knocking her backwards. She landed with a grunt, tumbling around to her feet.

"Cyril has done some more analysis on Demarcus and his speed. I think if he runs counter-clockwise to the sphere around the compound, it will hold the rip in place. At least temporarily. Then if we can get the power shut down in the basement, it should close the rip fully. Oh, wait . . ."

Mercury got knocked backwards but used his momen-tum to spring off the wall fragment that Sarah Jane hid be-hind and struck with a wicked downwards swing. "No waiting. Waiting isn't good right now," he spat.

"There needs to be a feedback loop through the rip as

well. Demarcus could get across from you and the two of you-"

"Sorry to interrupt," Demarcus grunted. "But how can I keep the rip from growing and do the feedback loop at the same time? I'm fast, but not that fast." He zipped back and forth, unable to keep in one spot for long.

"That is a problem." Liz sounded defeated, which didn't match her usual chipper optimism at all.

You were made to shine.

Lily thought of the words that came to her over the last year as she used her gift. For whatever reason, God had a purpose in giving this ability to a frightened girl. She had to be bold enough to shine when called upon.

"I think I can help," Lily called out. "Demarcus, can you get me opposite Mercury? I think my powers will interact with the stave. Then you can go keep us from exploding, or whatever."

"Are you sure about that? There's not much space over there." She could hear the worry in his voice. It warmed her heart that her boyfriend was so thoughtful, but she knew he struggled with leaving her in God's hands.

She tried to swallow, but her dry throat gave her little to work with. "We've got to try. Get the pulsar stave back to Mercury, get me in position, and go be a speed freak."

Before she could blast another wire, his strong arms gathered her and she flew across the room. Her hair splayed around her face as she tried in vain to brush wisps away. *When will I remember to keep a ponytail holder with me?*

"You good?" His dark eyes searched hers. Strength and concern radiated from them.

She gave him a quick peck. "All good. Go save the day."

After his goofy grin subsided, he dashed away.

"I can't really see you over there, Lily. Are you in position?" Mercury came over the line.

She braced her legs for balance. "I'm set. I think if you shoot a bolt my way, I can circle it back to the other stave. Have one in each hand and we'll try it."

"I don't want to fry a teenager from another dimension. It's bad for publicity. You sure about this?"

"Send it."

A bolt of lightning came blazing her way. This was a new trick—bending the light back around the other side of the orb. The light dazzled in an arc in front of her.

Then she heard Mercury scream.

Chapter Twenty

Iggy Risner

"Okay, so imagine you're in our shoes—except, replace the shoes with sneakers that are two sizes too small. Yep, that's how this adventure is rolling, folks. But hey, where would be the fun if things went smoothly, right? Keep your fingers crossed, we might just make it out in one piece!"

My frustration simmered, bubbling within me like a pot about to boil over. Mercury ordered Demarcus to pull us out of Site 17, and since Demarcus was a speedster I couldn't really get away. Outdoors now, removed from the epicenter of action, my annoyance grew. Couldn't they see that we were seasoned veterans of our neighborhood, that we were the saviors of Whispering Pines, a suburban neighborhood where much scarier things roamed?

Demarcus slipped an earbud my way, his low voice assuring me he'd give the signal when it was time for Oz and me to burst forth like avenging heroes. Yet, as we stood there, Oz's voice, like a relentless mosquito, persisted. His ceaseless inquiries drilled into my head, a persistent drip in the cavern of my thoughts.

"Iggy, you ever wonder why they left us out here? Do you think it's some kind of monster rumble? Like, a giant mutant squirrel taking on a three-headed snake? Oh, and Iggy, are these earbuds like super-secret spy communication devices?"

"Oz, quiet!" I urged, straining to listen in on the ongoing battle. The battle inside resonated through the panes, crashes and thuds punctuating with Mercury's sharp screams.

"But, Iggy, what if it's a colossal alien snail? One that leaves behind these sparkly trails, like a slimy rainbow?"

My hand clamped over Oz's mouth, a desperate attempt to stem the flow of words. The combat inside intensified, and I strained my ears for Demarcus's voice amidst the sounds. It didn't sound as if it was going well. Then, it struck me—we might be needed inside.

I released Oz. "Oz, I think we need to go back in."

Eyes wide, he asked, "But what about the ginormous snail?"

"Forget the snail. There is no snail. You got any of that strawberry wind soda left?"

His disappointed shake of the head told me all I needed to know. "No, I chugged the last one a little bit ago."

Oz hiked his leg up, squeezed his face tight. "Nope, nothing stinky left Iggy. I'm toot-free."

Just then, Liz's voice hummed in our ears. "Iggy, Oz, do you copy?"

I pressed the ear bud close to my ear. "Any idea how this thing works, Oz?"

"Just talk," Liz said. "Listen, don't go inside. That's not where we need you. We have a different mission."

"A mission?" I asked. "Like what?"

"Proceed down the hallway to your left. Near the end you'll find a shaft in the floor. Climb down the ladder and move to the end of the basement. Your task is to pull the lever, shutting down the reactor. You'll have to worm your way through debris and crawl through a cramped tunnel."

"Got it," I said. "And don't worry. We'll save them." Liz giggled and left the chat. I was pretty sure she was impressed with me.

"What did she say?" Oz asked.

"We need to head down to the basement," I said.

"The basement?" Oz cried. "Nope, sorry. I'm out."

"Oz, Mercury needs our help. We need to go down there and pull a lever in order to shut down the reactor."

"Did you not hear what I said about giant mutated squirrels?"

"Oz! There is no mutated squirrel!"

"That's what you said about the Brokken," Oz yelled. "Remember him! He was the big hairless Sasquatch we encountered when visiting Area 51 with Mom and Dad."

"Oz, that was Area 51," I yelled. "This is California. Normal people live here."

"Actually that's not entirely accurate," Liz said. I forgot she was listening.

"Iggy," Mercury's voice came over the ear bud. "Let me talk to Oz."

I handed the ear bud to Oz. "It's Mercury. He wants to talk to you."

Oz grabbed the earbud, stuck his tongue out at me, then slipped it in his ear. He nodded along for several seconds before standing straight and saying "Yes, sir!"

He slipped the ear bud back in my hand. "Come on, Iggy."

"What did he say?"

"He said you're scared of the dark and I needed to protect you."

"I'm not scared of the dark," I said, shoving the ear bud back into my ear.

"Iggy, you sleep with a night light. Now come on."

"I don't sleep with a night light," I said. "You do."

"If you two could hurry this up, I would really appreciate it," Mercury said. I thought I heard the same tone Mom gave us when we were goofing off in the grocery store.

We ventured down the hallway. Flashlights in hand, we stepped into the inky abyss of the entrance. The remnants of the past cluttered the area, and with each step, the erratic thudding of my heart echoed like an urgent drumbeat.

Oz's voice wavered, "Iggy, what if this stuff comes to life? Like, what if these old newspapers transform into paper beasts that start chasing us?"

Suppressing my sigh, I muttered, "Oz, seriously. They won't. Now keep moving."

At last, we faced the lever, its allure dampened by the pile of junk obstructing our way.

"Oh, come on now, you're probably thinking, 'These guys can't catch a break, can they?' Well, dear reader, let me assure you—this isn't just bad luck, it's a certified adventure! Now, where were we? Oh right, adventure!"

Undaunted, we plowed through, determined to create a path that even a blindfolded squirrel would appreciate. And then, out of nowhere, a colossal crash echoed above, sending Oz rocketing into the air like a startled cat. His expression, once rife with childhood innocence, now resembled a canvas painted with the surreal hues of disbelief.

"Time to hustle," he quipped, his voice jittery like a rabbit in a sudden spotlight.

And in a flash, the lights winked out, enveloping us in

an abyss so consuming, you could practically chew on the darkness. Oz clung to me like a leech on bare skin. His grip conveyed dozens of emotions ranging from impending doom to mild annoyance.

"Iggy, what if something else is in here? You know, something slithery and slimy, like a goop monster from an '80s movie?"

"Oz, let's be real. It's most likely a minor glitch," I said, desperately trying to sound as brave as the heroes in our comics. "And you don't know anything about 80's movies. Focus on the lever—we've got a job to finish."

We pressed on, our jittery hands engaged in a cautious dance with the debris. Our flashlights carved out paths in the dark, illuminating the world around us in feeble slices. And then, like a crescendo building to a climax, we reached the lever, our fingers tentatively outstretched, poised to seize the moment. But just as the tension seemed to reach its peak, another tremendous crash erupted above us, a rumble that ricocheted through the concrete ceiling like a quake of uncertainty. Oz's voice quavered once again, "Iggy, maybe it's time we seriously consider the term 'speed-run.'"

And then, without warning, both of our flashlights blinked out and darkness enveloped everything, swallowing us whole like a curtain descending on a scene-stealing act.

Chapter Twenty-One

Harry Wales

As Harry disentangled his limbs from that Dominic guy, Dr. Wayland seemed to grab the freaking *air between them* and pulled. The space in front of him seemed to open like a set of blinds being tugged by the cord. A swirling picture gapped in that space now. Purple lightning jolted through and knocked the two of them back.

Harry so wanted to just port back upright, but he still wasn't sure how his power would work interacting in this dimension. He pushed himself up and saw more craziness deep within the rip. A flying airship. The peaceful mangrove with water rippling around it.

Then his heart nearly froze.

A being made of smoke with electrical trails winding around it turned and looked at someone. Was that . . . the *Hoshek?* The supernatural being they'd defeated on the Golden Gate Bridge months ago? The thought of that evil entity taking over Harry's will made him cower.

"Harry, duck!"

A light pulsed behind him and Harry had the sense to dive to his left. Dominic used his arm bands to shoot crackling light at the rip. Sparks erupted as the two collided and the rip seemed to, well, zip itself back up.

Dominic ran to him and helped him upright. "I've done a lot of dimensional traveling. That wasn't showing us the present—it was showing possibilities. Don't let whatever you saw affect you."

Nodding, Harry untangled his robe at his legs. Oh man, a tear. His parents would ground him for a week if they had to pay the fee for it being damaged. As he shook himself free, he noticed a familiar warmth begin to return to his extremities.

Before he could consider this, Dr. Wayland split into two again. His copies pulled Harry and Dominic apart. Harry was thrown to the ground. When he rolled up, he saw Dominic in a chokehold. His Wayland seemed more . . . solid than the one coming at Harry again. Maybe the power was split between the two, or copies weren't as good as the original.

Hey, Steve . . . Harry chuckled at the old Michael Keaton movie that popped into his head.

"I'm so tired of you Procyon hacks pushing me to the side, ignoring what I've done! Don't you see? I've stabilized the Interstice. We don't have to fear it anymore—we can use it!"

As Dr. Wayland swung wildly, Harry dodged and ran for Dominic. "I don't know you, man, but I'd say there's something to fear. It's messed with your head."

Dominic's eyes were starting to roll back when Harry reached him. This Wayland's eyes had some weird purple glow. This was getting too freaky. It made Harry realize how much he appreciated his friends. He reached out and just made contact with Dominic's arm when a purple beam enveloped him and froze him in mid-motion.

The Waylands had folded together. The combination or the rip must be giving him more power. Harry couldn't even move his eyes with whatever this ray did. However, being in contact with Dominic anchored him to reality in a way he hadn't felt since the soda museum. When his powers were normal, not glitching.

Which meant he may have a way out of this predicament.

A familiar warping of the air took him and Dominic away from Wayland and deposited them several yards away. Dominic gagged and vomited. That's weird. Usually the first teleport made people sick, but Harry assumed if Dominic could move through dimensions, it wouldn't bother him.

A cry escaped from Dr. Wayland, who had dropped to

his knees. The sound tore through Harry's skull as he squeezed his hands against his ears, trying to dampen it. Dominic was similarly affected.

"It hurts. I don't know how long I can keep this up. When will Procyon see and send me the help I need to keep this stabilized?" Wayland cried. The poor man was delusional from his time here. Had he even had a chance to eat? That would drive Harry nuts.

Dominic wiped his sleeve across his mouth. "Thanks for that, I think."

"Can we leave now? I can control my teleportation more when I'm near you, but I can't sense how to get back to my friends."

He gestured towards Wayland. "I don't think just yet. Wayland seems to be the nexus. He's part of the reason the rip in my dimension is open and causing crazy things to happen."

"Like fighting a possessed soda machine?" Harry blurted.

Dominic furrowed his brows and frowned. "That's a new one . . ."

"Sorry, that's not the point. So you're saying we have to get Wayland out of here to help everything go back to normal?"

"That's my theory. I think if we work together, we can pull him free. Just try to stay tethered to me, and when I get my Echo Watches activated our combined abilities may yank him free."

A crack of thunder sounded. Only it wasn't from a cloud, but another time-space rip tearing into this reality. Wayland moaned, "You can't do that. You'll destroy every-thing!" In the purple swirling haze Harry could see Lily straining while bending a circle of light. Demarcus ran faster and faster around a building. Mercury screamed in agony. Was he dying? But he couldn't see Sarah Jane. Where was she?

His face flushed with the thought something might have happened to his girlfriend. Dominic gaped at the sight through the portal. "Mercury?" he called.

Wayland reached into the portal and caused some sort of electricity to start pulsing through the room that held Mercury and Lily. Now they both cried out.

"Whatever you're thinking, we'd better do it now." Harry gulped.

Dominic Zein

This has to end.

"Doctor Wayland!" I shout. "You can't do what you're planning to do."

"How do you know? You have no idea what I've sacrificed to make this possible!" Wayland's voice reverberates off invisible walls, as if we're standing in a massive auditorium, but he won't remove his hands from the rip. His gaze locks on me, full of violet fire. "Procyon *never* understood my passion. If they'd supported me, if they'd just *listened*, they wouldn't have to fear the Interstice, but learn to use it."

"I know you wanted to do good, Doctor, but what you're doing now is the opposite. There has to be a way for us to achieve your goals but end the strife your actions are causing." He has to stay focused on me. He can't pay attention to Harry, who is walking a slow, stealthy circle around to the other side of the rip—if something as two- or three-dimensional as a "side" applies in this place. "I can take you home."

It may be a lie. I hope we can separate Wayland from the rip. I hope we can do so without hurting him or even killing him. But I am more sure that if either of those possibilities conflict with what I have to do, I won't hesitate to sacrifice him.

This is what I do now. I redirect people's lives. I end them.

My role in the cold war between nearly identical dimensions isn't a bloodless one. I've removed people from Earth and taken them back to an alternate version because they were doppelgangers intent on harming others—doppelgangers who had killed and replaced other people.

Some ended their lives rather than be taken.

I miss being an architect.

"Doctor Wayland." Harry disappears behind the savage energies writhing around the rip. He's nearly in place. "I can't promise you a reunion."

His face slackens. I thought perhaps that might be part of what drives him. I can't imagine being stuck in a place where only hours had passed for me but decades elapsed for everyone else. "Maggie . . ."

The word squeezes my heart. I've said the name before, that way. Not that exact name, of course, but *the* name. Jess. My one and only. When I was terrified I'd lose her forever.

I almost did.

"Doctor Wayland. Daniel. What the boy said is true." I take a deep breath. "It has been more than forty years since you disappeared and were presumed dead. I don't know what's happened to Maggie or the people you would have known. What I do know is you don't belong here. None of us do. Let us help you escape."

"I . . . Don't think I can. I don't think it wants me to leave." The purple in Wayland's eyes fades, just a bit, so I can actually see his irises.

"But you have a choice," I urged. "You can let go of this place and return to where you belong."

Harry is there. His silhouette appears through the swirling energies of the rip, beyond the semi-transparent images of Mercury and Lily grappling with the interdimensional fluctuations.

But the rip surges. Its edges grow dark. Purple lightning skitters out from its core, enveloping Wayland. He cries out until his voice goes hoarse and is replaced by deep, sonorous groans.

"Your world will be ours," he moans, "And all in it will meet the same fate as me."

Ours?

Mercury has told me of the Whisperer. Procyon's forces have faced him time and again. I barely recall his hideous strength from when I was corrupted to do his work opening a portal between two realms that should never have been joined.

I won't let that happen again.

"Harry!" I aim the Echo Watches and unleash their golden energies. They're usually quick bursts but something about the manipulated rip drags them out into undulating streams.

Harry's warbled shout answers me. For a moment I assume his attempt failed—until he appears in front of me. He's warped and stretched, much like Wayland was, except the Echo Watches encircle Harry with their light. Harry grows in stature until he's eight, ten, twelve . . .

twenty feet tall.

Tall enough he can put his massive hands on either side of the rip and push them together.

The rip violently contracts, but then shoves back, attempting to grow even larger.

Harry shouts in a thunderous parody of a teenager's voice. Wayland screams wordlessly at him as the purple energies flood his body, setting him aglow like a hot coal.

I don't dare let the Echo Watches down, no matter how my muscles burn and a sharp, biting cold ripples through my body.

Jess.

I can't save Daniel Wayland.

It's up to everybody else before it's too late.

Chapter Twenty-Two

Iggy Risner

Okay, dear reader! Listen up! You and I, we're pals, right? I know, I know you're worried about the real hero of this story. You've probably skipped right by those other few chapters to land right here. So, let's get real.

Life's got its dark corners, like that sock you lost under the bed ages ago. Spooky, I know. Look, I wish I could say I was the Bruce Wayne of this scenario, minus the million-dollar gadgets, but let's be honest—I'm kinda freaked out.

Oh sure, everyone's had their close calls with "monsters." Like when you launch yourself from bed to light switch, practically flying, 'cause you think the flick of a switch is like garlic to a vampire. Poof! No more monsters. But here at Site 17? Yeah, the monsters didn't get that memo. No light switch, no garlic. Just me and my . . . well, Oz!

Listen, I'm a Risner. We're practically the heroes of

Whispering Pines! Dad rules the HOA like Thor rules Asgard, just with fewer hammers and more lawn citations. You see I've got an image to maintain here. I can't let Oz report back that when our flashlights and comms had zipped out, I screeched and jumped into his arms.

Let me set the stage. Because that's not what happened. I just kept thinking what's the one thing Oz really needs right now? And then it hits me. He needs me to be the hero. That's why I jumped, to reassure him that his big brother was here. *Plus the dude needs a mint. Like, ASAP. His breath could slay a dragon. And not in the heroic way.*

"Iggy!" Oz hollered, his voice ringing through the dark. "Our lights are gone! What'd you do?"

"Me? Do I look like an electrician to you?" I snapped back, fumbling around, banging the flashlight against my palm.

"Iggy, man, this is it. I'm gonna be monster munchies!" Oz's voice quivered.

"Trust me, you're not on the menu," I reassured him. "We just gotta find that lever. I have a feeling that might be our only escape!"

"Escape? That lever is more like a door release for the boogeyman. I'm staying put."

I rolled my eyes. "Listen, Oz. Monsters are more afraid of you right now than you are of them. Trust me, if they got a whiff of your breath, they'd run."

"I am NOT a monster!" Oz retorted.

"I didn't say you were," I protested.

"Yeah, you said my breath stinks. And for that comment, I'm so telling Mom."

Ah, if only I could see. I'd find a wall to do the classic, theatrical facepalm against. Kids these days, am I right? I'm not sure you could understand. Maybe you can. Listen, ever been in a "We're-the-only-ones-who-can-save-the-day" situation? No? Well, you're missing out. And by "missing out," I mean "probably enjoying a far less stressful life."

"Oz, listen," I said, "You hear that noise above us?" I pointed up, as if the direction would mean anything in the dark. Thump-thump-bang! It was like Mercury and the gang were having a demolition derby up there. "I don't know what they're up to, but it can't be good. They need us to complete this mission."

"What do we do, Iggy?" Oz sounded shaky.

"Grab my hand," I told him, doing my best to sound like a fearless leader. "I'll go first, like a human shield. But, you know, with less armor. When we hit that lever, I'm yanking it down."

"Alright, Iggy," Oz said, squeezing my hand. Trust me, if you think holding your little brother's hand in the dark is awkward, try doing it while narrating your own life. The things I do for heroism.

We shuffled forward like two contestants in a three-legged race, except the prize was—hopefully—not being monster chow. Step by toe-stubbing step, we made it to where I thought the lever was. My hand finally grazed cold metal. "Found it!"

With dramatic flair worthy of a movie score, I yanked the lever down.

But there was no spotlight, no grand orchestra—instead, Oz's flashlight flickered to life. Talk about perfect timing.

For a split second, the beam caught the eyes of a rat right before he performed an Olympic-worthy leap onto my head. Oz let out a scream that could've shattered glass. "RAT ON YOUR HEAD, IGGY!"

And then he was gone, flashlight and all, leaving me in pitch darkness with my new, um, headpiece.

I danced a jig, knocking the rat off.

And to think, Oz calls himself my wingman. More like run-man, am I right?

Mercury Hale

Enough of that. The rip was becoming a pain.

Literally.

Lily's plan had worked. The pulsar stave's energies synced perfectly with whatever it was she was blasting through the rip and, between the two of us, we'd started shrinking the thing. I had one half of the stave in each hand. Lily was somehow bending the blast from the weapon back around the massive expanding rip to the *other* stave, joining us in a brilliant golden ring.

Kind of reminded me of a huge halo. Don't tell Ramos.

Whatever Liz's calculations thought the dual effect was supposed to do, it seemed to be working, because we were constricting the rip—until it started screaming again.

Then blinding, paralyzing bolts of energy shot out. The agony was unreal. It brought me to my knees. My throat went hoarse from yelling. Even worse was Lily's high-pitched screaming, but after a moment of being horror-struck that a young girl was getting hurt, my fear turned to anger, just like Yoda warned. Which a dim part of my brain told me was funny given I was getting a worse bit of lightning torture than Luke had at the Emperor's hands.

What would Ramos do?

Cliche, I know, especially if I'd substituted that with a certain somebody else's name, but that's where my brain was at. For obvious reasons.

I was not going to let Lily or Demarcus or Sarah Jane down. It was up to Dominic to save Harry.

I had to save everybody else.

The pulsar staves felt like they were as riled up as the rip, twisting in my hands, trying to break free. No idea whether that was a good thing or a bad thing. But I had to get a handle on the situation—literally.

I ground my teeth and pulled the halves slowly together. For two ends that were supposed to join, they sure didn't want to budge. "Lily! Lily, can you hear me?"

My shouts sounded shaky and way less than heroic, but thankfully the earbuds were still working. For a moment, all I got back were sobs. Then Lily's voice, shaky at first, came back, "I'm . . . I'm here."

"When I say so, pour everything you have into this link of ours. I mean everything."

"I don't know if I . . . I can." Her voice collapsed into cries again. "It hurts so much."

"I know it does, Lily. I know." My muscles felt like they were on fire. Smoke rose from my suit in hissing tendrils. Pretty sure the smell wrinkling my nose was my skin actually burning. But Loredana's face filled my head. "But we've got to do this. Everything you can. On my go."

"Okay. Okay."

The stave was almost there. Almost. I yelled and dragged the ends together. Sparks jumped from one to the other. Come on . . .

A crackling bolt struck me square in the chest. It rolled across my body, leaping between my limbs, coursing through my arms, setting every bone buzzing. The staves fell apart. I went to my knees . . .

Almost.

Sarah Jane's arms looped around me. "Hold on! I've got you!" She sounded terrified but from what I could see of her face, beneath red hair whipped by the rip's whirlwind, she was as determined as I'd ever seen from a Procyon security guard—or Loredana.

"Don't think I've got much in the tank, kid," I rasped.

"Yes you do. Because you're not alone. We're here with you. Demarcus is keeping the danger from spreading. Iggy and Oz are down below, working on the power problem. Harry and Dominic are fighting from the other side."

"That's a lot of hands but this thing—"

"It's nothing God can't handle." She closed her eyes and murmured so softly the words seemed to seep into my head—and my body.

Bit by bit, slowly and then rapid-fire, my muscles cooled. My skin smoothed. Burns faded. The pulsar stave's energy began coursing through me. Almost back. Did she do that? On her own?

Or was she as serious as Ramos when it came to what she believed?

"Mercury!" Liz's cry cut across our comms. "The boys did it! They cut the power!"

The containment field collapsed. The whirlwind ebbed.

The rip itself wobbled and became less tangible, like a movie trying to fade off the screen.

"Lily!" I cried. "Now!"

I slammed the pulsar stave pieces together and held on as a surge of power unlike anything I'd ever experienced bowled me over. It took every ounce of my concentration to stay upright.

Fingers crossed I wasn't gonna pass out.

Chapter Twenty-Three

Demarcus Bartlett

The wind whipping by Demarcus's ears drowned out any chatter from the earpiece. He didn't know if his running was doing any good, but the rip didn't extend past the facility, so he had to believe it was doing something. If only Mercury and Lily could keep the containment . . . whatever going, then hopefully this would be over soon.

The fatigue of not eating and even being in a different dimension forced him to dig deep. There was some kind of resistance, a force pushing against him as he circled again and again. *God, if you're king of the universe, then you are in charge here too. Help us stand strong.*

A huge blast of energy created shock waves from the building outward. The force of it threw Demarcus off his feet. His momentum carried him through the air until he bounced several times into the brush. He just missed crashing into one of the SUV's. Even then, his whole body hurt with the impact.

Groaning, he tried to push himself up. His arms gave out and he slumped back down. Blackness started coming over his vision when two high-pitched voices grew closer.

"Demarcus? Did you feel that whoosh? Don't tell me you had Strawberry Wind again."

"Iggy, I told you I drank the last of it. Besides, it doesn't smell horrible out here."

Two sets of hands grabbed Demarcus's arms and yanked. The darkness retreated and his head cleared. Iggy and Oz pulled him to a kneeling position, where he could shake his head and clear the cobwebs that seemed to fill his skull.

"Thanks guys. Did you cause that power surge?"

The two clamored to talk at once, but Iggy managed a hand over Oz's mouth for a moment to speak clearly. "I think so! We pulled the power switch down a tunnel, and then we felt this huge air blanket squoosh us for a second. Then our flashlight came on and we rushed out to save you."

"My flashlight!" Oz cried as he wormed free from his brother's grasp. "You should have seen the rat on Iggy's head."

A rat? Demarcus wasn't afraid of much, but rodents freaked him out. Before he could comment, a bunch of noise squeaked through the bud in Iggy's ear. Where was his? It must have flown out in his crash.

"What's going on?"

Iggy squinted, trying to focus on the noise. "They're yelling about Lily?"

Oh no.

"Stay here!" he ordered, then he got up on wobbly legs and dashed in as fast as he could go. He collided with one wall due to his shakiness, but then he entered the chamber where the rip had been pulsating just minutes ago.

Sarah Jane and Mercury knelt by Lily. Smoke rose from her bright red hands and her head lolled back. "Lily?" he cried.

Sarah Jane's voice rang out with a strength and force he hadn't heard from her before, claiming promises and proclaiming healing. Lily's skin dulled to her normal color, and in a moment she gasped before slowly raising her head.

"Take it easy," Mercury said in the most soothing voice Demarcus had heard from the guy. "Those heroic near-death experiences aren't something to just jump up from."

So the dude wasn't only sarcasm and slinging a lightning staff.

Sarah Jane gave Lily a knowing smile. "She wasn't close to being dead. Just a little fried. At least it wasn't her brain this time." Mercury cocked his head at that. Demarcus had to laugh at the way forming holograms with her special gloves scrambled Lily's thoughts.

"Did we do it? Is the portal closed?" Her voice sounded hoarse, but they'd all been worse for wear before.

Mercury stood quite slowly. It looked like some steam rose from his costume as well. "It looks like it. I guess I could check in." He took out his earbud and held it so all could hear from it. "Liz, can you read me?"

"Well that was something. Even Cyril can't make heads or tails of it. If this event pushes him to a never-ending loop, I'm going to seriously complain to procurement about that extra fan he needs for —"

"Liz! Not the time. What's the status of the rip?"

A huff sounded through the earpiece. "It looks like all the tachyon readings have settled to baseline levels. No other irregular signals coming in from Site 17. I have one question. Why do the readings on Garvey and the security team show they're in a REM state?"

The teens all laughed, and even Mercury shook his head and chuckled. "Maybe we can show Procyon a demonstration sometime. One more thing, do you have a lead on Dominic and Harry?"

If the rip was contained, shouldn't that help Harry? Demarcus glanced around, hoping to see Harry's goofy grin pop up at any second.

Nothing came from the earpiece. After a minute, Mercury had to speak up. "Liz, do you have anything?"

Her voice was hushed. "I don't have anything on them. Not even on the tracker we sent with Dominic.

"I'm sorry."

Dominic Zein

All that struggle and it cuts off as if someone's flipped a light switch.

The rip collapses, as does Wayland. He falls onto his hands and knees, gasping like a marathon runner just short of the finish line. There's no evidence left of the catastrophic rip between dimensions except a faint ripple that fades away while I blink. It could have been nothing more than an afterimage.

"Is it gone?" Harry's on the ground, too, and he's returned to his normal size, though there's a thin golden aura about him. I'm assuming that will fade as well, but then again, I've never seen the Echo Watches do what they just did. Harry's hair is plastered to his skull by sweat. "Did we seal it?"

"I think so—at least from our side of the problem. Doctor?" I say to Wayland. "Daniel? Are you all right?"

He lifts his face. I can't help but recoil. Wayland's features are blurred with every move he makes. The man seems out of sync with his surroundings. Worse, his eyes are still glowing a brilliant purple, and there's three of them. They deepen past violet into a deep, pulsating red.

"What did you do?" His voice shifts between a snarl and a whisper. "I can't feel it anymore. There's no—connection. Something's wrong."

"Daniel." I hold out a hand. The air around us begins to vibrate. Is that wind howling nearby? I hear a distant peal of thunder. "Come with us. We know people who can help you. Let's see what they can do for you, all right?"

"But . . . Maggie."

"I don't know what's happened to her or where she's gone. Come with me and I promise you we can try to find out."

Wayland's face contorts into a warped grimace. His face looks—bigger. Grayer. A purple sheen forms on his hair and hands. "She thinks I'm dead. I'd been dead."

"No, Daniel, we—"

"I am dead." He tilts his head back and screams. It's a cry of sorrow and anguish, rising in pitch. My heart aches for him . . .

Until the pitch keeps rising and his cry becomes a hideous shriek.

Harry yelps. "Um, Dominic?"

The ground beneath us is cracking. I look down at my reflection as fissures form across a glassy surface. That surface is becoming more and more transparent with each passing second. There's a storm-ravaged landscape far below, one thrashed by violet thunderstorms. Sharp gray mountains reach for the sky. More piercing screams compete with the thunder for our attention.

I recognize the landscape. Cold sweat breaks out on my face and my hands.

The Interstice.

It's coming for us.

"Doctor, please!" I shout over the booming sounds. I take a step toward him. The same cracks appear on a distant horizon around us. They're getting nearer after every breath. "We have to go!"

"I can't . . . I can't . . . leave." His voice is a warped parody of what it should be. If the distortion keeps up I won't be able to understand him. Teeth spread and lengthen in his mouth. His body bulges, muscles tearing through his clothes. Flesh blackens. But even as his red eyes bulge, tears drip freely. "If I do, it will come with me."

"Maybe we can stop whatever's coming." Harry trembles but he stands beside me, ready for—this. He looks up at me, eyes wide with both fear and innocence. "Right?"

He's brave. I'll give him that. I can't help wishing my son—if I ever have one—will face the dangers that are out there like Harry does. But he doesn't yet understand. There's more nuance, more complexity, more *darkness* to the world than he realizes. There's two sides to everything and everyone.

Even me.

I touch his shoulder. Pieces of what I assumed were the horizon crumble, revealing swirling storm clouds. Our pocket dimension is falling apart. Time isn't on our side. The Interstice is devouring this plane. "On my signal, use your powers to return us to the Procyon Tracking center. I'll use the Echo Watches to stabilize our path, even though I won't be following the usual route."

"The usual—?"

"Trust me."

He stares at me a moment, then nods and takes a deep breath.

I look back at Wayland. Bulges appear in the blackened flesh that's broken through his sides and back. They twist and lengthen into tentacles, growing small spikes as they get bigger.

Few people even at Procyon Foundation know the truth behind the astral fiends. I never thought I'd see the transformation firsthand. All I can do is pray God will safeguard Wayland's soul. "I'm sorry, Daniel."

"I . . . am too. I should . . . have known better." His face is almost completely alien, flattening and broadening as his head compresses onto his neck. "But he . . . he can't be allowed out."

The storm blasts through the remainder of our pocket

dimension, scattering its ethereal beauty in a last thunder-strike. Harry and I cling to each other, buffeted by winds, with only the shuddering ground beneath us. It's nearly faded.

"Go!" Wayland shrieks. "And . . . forgive me!"

"Harry!" I cry out.

Harry screams something, and as I fire up the Echo Watches, a golden light envelopes us. It grows brighter and brighter until everything washes out in a brilliant white blaze. A keening wail deafens me.

There's nothing.

Silence, and warmth, and stillness. It holds us until my heart stops racing. There's no resisting the sense of peace. I can't see Harry but I feel his hands. His pulse slows, too.

Peace.

Then a crack like a final thunderbolt. My legs collapse. The space around us is cool and dark, except for the glow from . . . screens? Lightbulbs?

Pink hair?

My knees hit the floor. I wince.

Harry whoops beside me, arms upraised. "We did it! We're back!" But he puts his hand to his mouth, curtailing his celebration, and doubles over. Vomits. The stink reaches my nose a second later.

I shake my head and chuckle. Yes, we're back.

"Dominic!" Liz Stojan crouches beside me, her hands

pressed together, her eyes full of tears. She reaches for her tablet. "Mercury, can you hear me? Dominic and Harry are . . . I've got them! They're safe. Oh wow. Are you guys okay?"

I try not to think about what Daniel Wayland gave up in his pursuit of powers he didn't understand—what he became in the end. "I think," I manage to croak, "we will be."

Chapter Twenty-Four

Iggy Risner

Here is the thing about Top Secret! It means you are important. This mission was something both Oz and I would never have the chance to talk about. If the folks in the suburbs knew what just happened at Site 17 they would panic! Bunkers would be dug, pantries stocked, and every kid would be stuck eating freeze dried Brussels sprouts!

Ugh!!!!

So, the world can never know. Now I just needed to find a way to bribe Oz into keeping his mouth shut!

"Iggy, Oz." I turned around and noticed Mercury along with the others coming our way.

"Hey, Mercury," I said.

"Remember what we discussed," he said. "You can write this down in your case files, but not a word."

"So you are asking him to keep a secret from their parents?" Demarcus asked, smiling.

"I'm not allowed to keep secrets from Mom," Oz said. "She says that's like telling a lie."

Mercury pinched the bridge of his nose.

"Oz and I will discuss it," I said. "No one will find out."

Oz crossed his arms and gave Mercury a hard look.

"Thank you," Mercury said. He turned to walk away before spinning back. "Oh, Garvey is driving you back. Just make sure neither one of you drinks any Strawberry Wind."

"No problem," I said. "I think we are fresh out."

"Good," Mercury smiled and shook his head. "You two did good out there. We wouldn't have made it if you hadn't braved the tunnel and flipped that switch."

My face burned. "Thanks, Mercury!"

Mercury walked away and Demarcus stuck out his hand. "I guess this is goodbye."

"Yeah," I said. "If you are ever in Edmond, Oklahoma, stop by Whispering Pines and say hi."

"I don't know if Edmond, or even Whispering Pines, exists in our dimension."

"Oh, right!" I had forgotten Demarcus and the others had traveled from some other place.

"But, if I ever accidentally travel through a rip again, I'll look you up."

"Well, you're always welcome in Whispering Pines. You'll love it. I'm sort . . . I'm sort of the hero there."

Demarcus laughed, shook my hand, and left. A number of emotions washed over me. They all headed back inside Procyon and I watched as my friends disappeared through the door. The knot in my stomach tightened, and a lump formed in my throat. After everything we'd just been through, saying goodbye felt like tearing a piece of my heart away.

In the black SUV, silence enveloped us like a heavy fog. I stared out the window, the passing landscape a blur of greens and blues. We'd been up all night, and Oz's snores filled the air, a stark contrast to the tension inside the vehicle. Garvey's grip on the steering wheel was tight, his jaw clenched. Each bend and curve in the road seemed to mirror the twists in our emotions.

We pulled into the campground, and I nudged Oz awake.

"I don't want to eat the carrots . . ." Oz said as he lifted his eyelids. "Iggy?"

"We're back at the campsite." I pointed at Mom and Dad's RV. Garvey opened the door and we both slid out.

A chilly wind blew through the trees and I hugged my chest.

"Your mom and dad will wake soon," Garvey said. "They won't remember much. We gave them an extra dose of juice so they would stay sedated a bit longer. Kinda had to after word got out you two had managed to stow away in the back on the way to the site."

"Oh, yeah," Oz said. "Sorry about gassing you and the rest of the watchmen."

"Watchmen?" Garvey said.

Oz shrugged. "Yeah, we have guys like you back in Whispering Pines. They are the neighborhood watchmen."

Garvey closed his eyes and took a deep breath. He smiled. "Don't worry about the gassing, kid. But do me a favor."

"Sure," I said. "Anything."

"Don't ever bring that soda around me again," Garvey smiled. "Worst thing I've ever smelled."

I laughed. "You're okay, Mr. Garvey."

"Say," Garvey said. "You wouldn't happen to have an extra can would you?"

"No," I said. "But they have some at the soda museum."

"Hmm," he shook his head. "I'm thinking Mercury needs to get a whiff of that sometime. Anyway, kids, you better get inside before your mom and dad wake. It's been a pleasure."

"Thanks, Mr. Garvey," I said. "If you are ever in Whispering Pines, stop in and say hello."

"Doubtful, kid," he said and then turned and left.

"Iggy," Oz said.

"What is it?"

"I'm tired."

"Yeah, me too."

After all, saving the world takes a lot out of you.

Mercury Hale

I watched from the windows of one the elevated walkways connecting the Procyon towers, arms folded, as a black SUV rolled out of the parking lot. "That worked out."

"Worked out?" Dominic frowned at me. "Did you understand what I told you about Doctor Wayland? What happened to him?"

I shivered. Yeah, I understood, all right, and I'd known it was a possibility ever since the extradimensional being Tenebrae had revealed a bunch of secrets about the war that tore apart my home world. "I meant, none of us died, and the really bad idea of taming a rip didn't result in our dimension shredding itself."

"Oh." Dominic's expression eased. "When you put it that way . . ."

"What happened to Wayland was . . . No joke, the worst thing I can imagine happening to anyone. But we'd better make sure the truth gets into Procyon's permanent files so that everyone going up against our enemies knows how easily they could get seduced by the same power."

"Insightful, Mercury."

"Hey, I'm taking whatever wins I can." I shook my head. "Definitely not gonna make a habit out of this."

"Out of what?"

"Are you serious?" I raised an eyebrow. "Babysitting."

Dominic smiled. "I think you handled it pretty well."

"Thanks for the vote of confidence. I'll let you know whether it's worth it once I hear back from the bosses."

"Mercury, let me tell you something I don't think anyone else has. Take it as advice from a friend who knows what he's talking about." Dominic put a hand on my shoulder. "The person who's hardest on you is you."

Heat rose to my face. I got it. I really did. It's not something easy to admit, but hearing it from a guy like Dominic—a guy who was one of the few who really understood what I'd been through—meant a lot more than trying to argue with my own snarky brain. "I appreciate it. Really."

"You're welcome. I think we had a real moment there. Maybe I should record it for posterity."

I smirked. "Don't push it, man, or I might knock you on your posterity."

Someone softly cleared her throat. Lily, Demarcus, Sarah Jane, and Harry were standing at the far end of the hall. They'd put their Renaissance faire costumes back on so they could look just as geeky going back to their home dimension as they'd been when they left, except Harry's robes were more ragged than the rest owing to his tussle in Wayland's pocket dimension. "You guys ready?" I asked.

"Think so." Demarcus stepped forward and offered his hand. We shook. "Thanks for everything."

"Thanks? To me?" I chuckled. "There's way too much of that going around. I'm the one who owes all of you guys the bigger debt. Whatever it is that gives you your powers, you deserve them. That other San Francisco you come from is lucky."

Demarcus scratched the back of his neck and became super interested in his shoes, but Lily took his place with a smile as bright as ever. "I think we were meant to be here. That's what John taught us."

"To be of service wherever we can," Sarah Jane said.

I gave them both thumbs up. Seriously, I was all out of pep talks. Enhanced healing aside, I was exhausted and ready to get away from everybody.

My phone buzzed. Loredana checking in. Well, almost everybody.

"Good luck, kids." I shook hands with all of them. Lily came back and gave me a big hug, which made me blush even more than Dominic's heartwarming bro talk. "Dominic and Liz have everything figured out, I think. Right?"

"We do." Dominic pointed at Harry. "This one and I make a pretty good team."

Harry turned beet red. "Yeah. Um. I think we do."

"Nice. One thing, though." I pulled the pulsar stave from my belt, where I'd tucked it in its compact form. "This. And you."

Demarcus looked around, then poked his own chest. "Me?"

"Yep. Liz informs me there's no reason she can pin down as to why you were able to activate the stave." I glanced at Lily. "Or why your powers synced with it so neatly."

The teens shared guilty but happy looks, like they had a secret they weren't willing to share. "I'm gonna call it God's mysterious ways and leave it there," Demarcus said.

I wasn't sure about his analysis but, hey, I wasn't about to knock the possibility. Ramos had shown me more than enough possibilities for me to stay open-minded. "Maybe we'll chat about it some other time."

"Maybe."

"Definitely maybe!" Liz came jogging up from behind them. She pressed between the kids. "Oh, good. Everybody's still here. I was hoping you hadn't left because I figured out a way to modify that tachyon dowser Mercury used a while back to track people outside our dimension and it took me a while to fiddle with it during the crisis but it's just a prototype—"

"Liz!" The Anointed called her name in unison.

Dominic and I burst out laughing. We were still wiping

tears away when Liz continued with, ". . . And it won't require much charging. There's a tiny battery in there that, um, isn't strictly legal in terms of national security . . ."

I held up my hand. "Just. Don't."

"Sorry." Liz winked at the kids. She handed the small black oval to Lily, who turned it over. A silver Procyon emblem gleamed on it.

"Nice." Harry said. "But does it really need the logo?"

"Why not?" I shrugged. "You guys don't have a Procyon Foundation on your world."

The teens gave each other curious looks.

My smile faded. "Do you?"

"Um, we've never heard of one," Sarah Jane said.

I looked over my shoulder at Dominic. "Is there?"

"I have no idea. The alternate Earth I've been to has a version, so, I suppose it's a possibility," he said.

"Liz?"

She chewed her lip. "Oh. Well . . . I don't think so. Probably not?"

"Alrighty." A headache was lurking behind my eyes so I did what I do best—mentally told myself *Nope* and ignored the potential problem. "See you, kids."

Dominic and Liz ushered the Anointed from the walkway. Harry sidled up to Dominic and murmured, "Before we go home, do you think we could make a quick stop?"

I didn't find out where he wanted to go sightseeing because the doors shut them off from me and I let out a big sigh. Finally.

The phone buzzed again. I answered this time. "Sorry, Loredana. I was just cleaning up."

"Quite reassuring to hear." She sounded tired, but in a good mood, which made me feel a ton better. "Liz has kept me apprised of the unfolding situation. I'm in the midst of a detailed after-action report for Mr. Alvarez that requires your considerable input."

"Oh?" I grinned again. "How considerable?"

"Considerable enough I shall require full restocked snacks and extensive cuddling as we watch a terrible saccharine Hallmark movie."

"Multitasking. Sweet."

"How did you fare?"

"With the mission? Like I told Dominic, not too—"

"With the children."

Ah. Figured that's what she was aiming for. Couldn't imagine why she had kids on the brain. "You know, it wasn't too bad. I kind of liked them."

"Kind of?"

"Okay, they were pretty great. I . . . had fun. Mostly."

"Jolly good. I'm delighted to hear you don't find children detestable. It will serve you well fairly soon."

A strange, flipping sensation tickled my stomach. The date was approaching. Soon enough, it wasn't going to be the two of us.

It was going to be the four of us.

"Can I expect you home posthaste and with my snacks?" she asked. "We can talk about it then."

"Are you kidding? Of course I'll bring the snacks" My stomach grumbled so loudly I thought she'd be able to hear it through the phone. "Besides, I've got to get out there and get another pizza."

Chapter Twenty-Five

Demarcus Bartlett

Dominic led them to the garage where another SUV awaited them.

"Are we going to the park where we first arrived?" Demarcus asked.

"First I have one detour and then we'll swing over to the park. Swing, get it?" Dominic grinned.

"Do you have kids?" Lily replied.

"Not yet."

"At least your dad jokes are ready to go." That got a laugh from everyone, and Demarcus beamed at his girl-friend's quick wit being used on someone other than him.

A driver from the Procyon security detail waited in the vehicle. Dominic got in the front seat while they poured into the back two rows. Dominic gave the driver instructions then pulled out his phone. "Jess? Yes, I'm okay. Hold on." He tipped the phone away from his mouth. "Sorry, guys, I have to take this one. It's my wife."

As Dominic began talking to Jess, Lily and Sarah Jane turned towards the back to talk. Harry kept one eye out the window as the SUV exited the garage and roared towards a San Camillo highway.

"This is a new one for our scrapbook," Sarah Jane said. "I didn't ever think we'd travel to another dimension. I'm not even sure how to tell John about it. How do we begin to explain it?"

While Demarcus and Lily stared at each other, trying to figure out a response, Harry replied in a thoughtful tone. "God is the King over all the heavens. I'm not sure it's specified anywhere how many there are. I bet John will understand better than we think."

"And you're doing okay after being trapped in . . . what was it again?" Lily said.

"Apparently it's part of what Procyon calls 'the Interstice.' I popped into a couple of different areas when I first got there. I was trying to get out, but my powers were glitching still. There were some things that were terrifying, and others that were beautiful. I'm not sure I will ever fully understand it all."

Demarcus leaned back. The last twenty-four hours or so were a lot to take in. Oh snap, the curfew! Sweat broke out over his forehead as he thought about Mr. Beausoleil turning different shades of red when Lily got home late.

There was no good excuse either—he didn't think *we got sucked into a different dimension* would be the best reply.

"Uh, Demarcus? You look like you're getting sick. Do you need prayer?" Sarah Jane put a hand on his arm, ready to jump into action.

"Is everything all right back there?" Dominic was off the phone.

"I think I'm about to get Lily grounded for life. She had a curfew and we blew past it while trying to repair rips." Lily's eyes grew three sizes, her baby blues ready to glow with the shock of the thought.

Dominic chuckled. "That would be likely, except I think this time we're going to be okay. Normally when I travel dimensions, there's no aspect of time travel. However, I think with Harry's help in fine-tuning things, you'll arrive right when you left. It should be like you never left. Operative word, should."

That was reassuring. Demarcus took a couple of breaths to calm down.

"Are we here?" Harry nearly shouted in excitement. Guess he was ready to get out of this dimension. Except, there was no sign of a park outside. A lighted sign with a few broken bulbs flashed, "Carlito's."

"Here's our detour before we hit the dimensional highway. You can't leave San Camillo, or our Earth, without trying this."

Were they finally going to get some real food?

Dominic jumped out and returned with two boxes. Demarcus remembered the smell on Mercury when they first arrived and he had landed on some pizza boxes. His mouth wouldn't stop drooling. Could he have one pizza by himself?

"This is on me. I figured saving another world deserved something," Dominic said.

Demarcus almost groaned with his hunger. "Man, thank you so much. Two pizzas will really hit the spot."

"Uh, sorry. I figured one would do you guys. The other one is for Jess and I. She wanted me to pick up dinner."

Lily swatted at Demarcus. "We really appreciate it, even with our pig back here trying to hog it all. Smells so good."

Sarah Jane took a box from the front along with a pile of napkins, and the girls started handing out slices. Demarcus felt stupid from assuming, but Harry came to the rescue. "I was hoping for the same thing," he whispered.

A familiar park loomed on the right as they finished inhaling the pepperoni and cheese delights. Demarcus licked his fingers, earning another disapproving look from Lily. They tumbled out of the SUV and surveyed the crime scene tape surrounding the warped metal and plastic of the formerly possessed playground equipment.

Another silver SUV had pulled out a makeshift shaved

ice machine, with a couple of beefy dudes handing out free snow cones. Dominic pointed. "It's not quite a neuralyzer like the Men in Black used, but they're doing their best to create a distraction."

Sarah Jane burst out laughing. "You mean the super-secret monster hunting corporation has a snow cone division?"

Dominic shrugged and started to laugh as well. "I'd offer you one, but I'm not sure how well they would survive the trip."

A thought slugged Demarcus in the gut. "Wait, when I first teleported with Harry, I lost my lunch. Is that going to happen this time?" Not the delicious pizza!

After a moment, Dominic sighed. "Just a second." He jogged to their rig and returned with the second box. "I guess you won't be here anytime soon, and I can pick up a new one easily enough." He handed it to Demarcus.

"I didn't mean for you to give your pizza up."

Dominic gave his shoulder a light punch. "Two pizzas for saving our world. My final offer. This way, if you have any . . . issues, you can try it again."

They huddled up. "Thank you for helping us get home, and for saving Harry," Sarah Jane said. She blushed as she looked at Harry.

"Of course. It was an experience for sure. It was a pleasure meeting you guys. Who knows? I could end up in your dimension sometime. It will be your turn to find the pizza joint."

Lily wrapped her arms around Demarcus as Dominic held up his arms and the glowing bands—the Echo Watches?—began glowing and whirling. Harry held on to Dominic's arm and took Sarah Jane's hand. They all linked together, ready to head home.

In a swirl of light and wind, they found themselves in a foggy park. At least Demarcus's stomach didn't do flips. Dominic waved and disappeared again to avoid being seen in a foreign world. The four of them looked around as the mist dissipated almost as fast as it came on.

The Ren Faire continued as if nothing had happened. What a crazy time! Demarcus looked up to the sky and whispered a prayer of thanks that their God kept watch over them, even when hopping to different worlds.

They started walking towards a table when a guy dressed as a barbarian came up to them. He approached so suddenly, Demarcus noticed Lily flash a quick light before calming her power down.

"Where did you guys get that pizza? It smells out of this world!"

They all dropped to the ground, laughing hysterically.

The Authors

J.J. Johnson

J.J. Johnson is an award winning author who loves comic books, coffee, and writing fun adventure stories, including the award-winning Iggy & Oz tales. After giving up his dream of becoming a professional wrestler, he settled in Edmond, Oklahoma, with his wife, their two boys, a hyperactive dog, a cat who hates him, and a bunny who nibbles.

Jason C. Joyner

Jason is a physician assistant by day where he helps patients. By night he torments his characters and watches too much Star Wars. He's the author of the YA superhero series Rise of the Anointed, including the award-winning *Launch*.

Steve Rzasa

Steve Rzasa doesn't slay monsters, but he defeats word count goals. He's the author of several dozen novels, novellas, and short stories of science-fiction and fantasy, including the award-winning Mercury Hale series. When he's not writing, he's reading ... or planning the next adventure.

Acknowledgments

There's so many people we could thank for supporting our wacky endeavor, but here's a short list of the most important ones.

Ashley, Beccy, and Carrie—the wives of us guys, for putting up with our snickering Zoom calls and muttered brainstormings.

Kirk DouPonce of Dog Eared Designs for bringing our characters to life in an epic cover design.

Becky Dean, for being the fourth Musketeer of this epic crossover project by providing us with encouragement and, when necessary, threats.

Andi Gregory, for editing our work and ridding us of errors with professional flair.

The Masterminds: Josh Smith, Josh and Liberty Hardt, and Tina Gollings, for being there to keep us writing.

You're all tremendous.

- J.J., Jason, and Steve